LIGHTYEAR ENTERTAINMENT presents
a BENJAMIN MELNIKER-
MICHAEL E. USLAN PRODUCTION of
a JIM WYNORSKI film
starring LOUIS JOURDAN,
HEATHER LOCKLEAR,
SARAH DOUGLAS
and DICK DUROCK as SWAMP THING

PRODUCTION DESIGNER—ROBB WILSON KING, DIRECTOR OF PHOTOGRAPHY—ZORAN HOCHSTATTER, EXECUTIVE PRODUCERS—TOM KUHN AND CHARLES MITCHELL, WRITTEN BY DEREK SPENCER AND GRANT MORRIS, PRODUCED BY BENJAMIN MELNIKER AND MICHAEL E. USLAN, DIRECTED BY JIM WYNORSKI

A NOVEL BY PETER DAVID
BASED ON A SCREENPLAY BY DEREK SPENCER
AND GRANT MORRIS

THE RETURN OF SWAMP THING

A CORGI BOOK 0 552 13581 X

First publication in Great Britain

PRINTING HISTORY
Corgi edition published 1989

Corgi Books are published by Transworld Publishers Ltd., 61–63 Uxbridge Road, Ealing, London W5 5SA, in Australia by Transworld Publishers (Australia) Pty. Ltd., 15–23 Helles Avenue, Moorebank, NSW 2170, and in New Zealand by Transworld Publishers (N.Z.) Ltd., Cnr. Moselle and Waipareira Avenues, Henderson, Auckland.

Printed and bound in Great Britain by Cox & Wyman Ltd., Reading, Berks.

Dedicated to the dazzling imaginations of the people who spawned one of the most acclaimed characters in comics

THE RETURN OF
SWAMP
THING

I float . . . peacefully . . . in the womb of the . . . earth mother . . . feeling . . . nurtured . . . in the green.

I seem to recall . . . another time . . . such as this . . . when I hovered . . . newly formed within . . . a woman's body. But the woman was flesh . . . and blood . . . and tissue . . . throbbing and hot . . . not the peaceful cool nurturing . . . of the earth mother.

And I was taken . . . from the womb . . . to a world of . . . flesh . . . a world I left . . . in a burning symphony of pain.

I was hurled from that world . . . and want no part of it . . . for it wants . . . no part of . . . me.

There is pain there . . . and hurt . . . and memories . . . that give me . . . sadness . . . not like here . . . in the green.

Above me . . . is the peace of . . . the swamp. . . . I am one . . . with it . . . with the swamp. . . . I have no need for . . . earthly con-

cerns. Why should I . . . when my concern . . . is the earth . . . itself?

Let the flesh . . . go on about . . . its small concerns. I have no need . . . of the flesh. I have the dirt . . . and the grass . . . and the leaves. I need . . . nothing else.

I am . . . whole.

1

The doorknob came off in his hand.

Dr. Bernstein stood there a moment, glancing left and then right in embarrassment to see if anybody had spotted him. The screen door had started to open when he'd pulled it, but when the doorknob had abruptly detached itself, the door had swung shut again with a discomfiting *thwank.*

It should not have come as all that much of a surprise. When the cab had dropped him off at the front of the Wein Motel, the doctor's first assessment was that the entire structure might come tumbling down upon being nudged by even the lightest of breezes. It had the general appearance and ambience of the Bates Motel from *Psycho*—desolate and unappealing, the wood of its exterior staying together more out of habit than anything else, the nails having long since rusted away.

Indeed, perhaps the only reason it was still

standing was because no wind had come along to knock it over. The Wein Motel was situated directly at the edge of Suicide Swamp, deep in the heart of the Louisiana bayou. The air simply hung there, as if defying a stray zephyr to get it to move. No zephyr was willing to take up the challenge, apparently.

Bernstein had heard the expression "oppressive heat" but had never quite grasped the full meaning before this. He had wondered why the cabbie had snickered at his Brooks Brothers suit when he'd been picked up at the airport.

Now he understood. The humidity had reduced his fine clothes to little more than an eight-hundred-dollar damp rag. He'd removed his jacket, which had already soaked through, while his pressed slacks hung limply on him, his once crisp white shirt hugging him like a second skin. Sweat was dripping into his eyes, and he pulled at his tie, finally becoming so fed up that he yanked the tie off and tied it around his forehead. He looked like something out of a samurai film.

So there he stood with the doorknob in his hand, feeling foolish, and making some vague attempt to jam it back into the door. His airplane carry-on bag sat next to him on the porch of the motel. Directly to his right a VACANCY sign hung lopsidedly on the wall by one piece of fishline, the other piece presumably having snapped. Bernstein started to feel if he didn't get into some air-conditioning, he was going to be the next thing that snapped.

He heard a voice from inside ask, with what sounded like a British accent, "Knob come off again?"

Bernstein gave up the subterfuge. "I'm afraid so," he admitted. "I'll pay for the damage. . . ."

"Quite all right, old boy, quite all right. In you come, then."

The screen door leading to the lobby was opened from the inside. Bernstein peered in, his eyes trying to adjust to the dimness of the lobby. There wasn't all that much to see, really. A couple of rattan chairs, one with a hole in the seat, another with a hole in the back. A calendar on the wall turned to October of 1985. A painting of a creature that looked vaguely like a small white monkey, but with a distinctly sinister gaze to it. That was all.

Bernstein turned toward the desk and took an involuntary step back upon seeing the clerk who had let him in. The clerk was tall, almost cadaverous. His hair was long and black, coming to well beneath his shoulders, and he sported an equally shaggy beard. His eyes were sunken but extremely alert, with a gleam in them that hinted toward slight dementia.

"Aren't you hot with all that hair?" said Bernstein, who began to sweat even more just looking at him.

The clerk appeared to consider this. "I don't know. I've never been without it, so I have nothing to compare it to. Me name's Alan. You need a room?"

"Actually, I'm supposed to be meeting someone here. A Doctor Lana Zurrell?"

Alan paused a moment, looking Bernstein up and down. "Brit, like me? Black hair, sharp jaw, stare that would melt an iceberg?"

"Yes, that's her."

"Haven't seen her."

Bernstein blinked in confusion. "I beg your pardon?"

"I'm just yanking you, mate. She's in room 3A. Told me if a Doctor Bernstein came looking for her, I should send him over."

"That would be me."

Alan stared at him. "Pardon me for saying so, but . . . you don't look it."

Bernstein gave a small smile. "My father was Jewish. My mother was Japanese. You're looking at Wong Sing Bernstein . . . psychiatrist and acupressurist." And, as befitting his Japanese appearance, Bernstein bowed slightly at the waist.

Alan did not return the bow but merely stared at Bernstein with a most disquieting gaze. "Take a spot of friendly advice, Doc?"

"If I can."

"I've run this," and he made a vague, encompassing gesture, "establishment for quite a few years. Seen quite a bit of things, know all the stories. And I know things, see? I know that some bad things are going to be happening in the swamp very shortly."

"Now how would you know that?" asked Bernstein with professional patience.

"Here and there. Listen to the birds, listen to the 'gators . . . listen to what the weeds say as they rustle. What do you hear, Doc? Right now? This minute?"

Bernstein paused, tilting his head slightly. "Nothing."

"Exactly. Nothing. This time of day, flies are usually thick as . . . well, thick as flies." He leaned against the desk, his hair brushing against his elbow. "Should be buzzing enough to drive you off your nut. But even the flies know something's coming and are just talking quietly among themselves. That's why there's no noise. None of them, from the biggest reptile to the lowliest bug, wants to draw attention to itself."

Bernstein nodded, mentally classifying this desk clerk as someone who was in desperate need of therapy. Then again, considering the remoteness of the motel, it was a wonder he was sane at all.

"Everything's quiet . . . and the swamp man is listening. Don't you get it, Doc?" said Alan, and his voice became lower and darker. "This is his place. His place of power. And you should not have come here."

There was a dead silence then as, somewhere nearby, the flies muttered among themselves. Then Bernstein said, with a forced smile, "I'd like to thank you for sharing that with me. Now, if you'll excuse me . . ."

"And I'd stay away from that woman, Doc. She

looks like the type, if you paid her enough, she'd swallow a mouse."

"Thank you again. We'll talk more later." Bernstein bowed again slightly and walked back out the screen door, allowing it to *thwank* noisily shut behind him.

Alan watched him go and said in a low voice, "No . . . I don't think we will."

Bernstein walked along the side of the motel, each step sinking his patent leather shoes into the mud, as he checked the room numbers. He found 3A and stepped up, knocking softly on the door.

A sultry female voice called from within. "Come in. It's open."

Bernstein stepped in, shutting the door behind him.

He couldn't see anything. He moved toward the window to pull aside the drape, and then a small light came on next to the bed.

Illuminated by the light on the nightstand was Lana Zurrell. Bernstein's breath caught in his chest.

She lay stretched out on the bed, wearing the sheerest of pink nightgowns. Her head was propped on her hand, her luminous eyes watching him carefully.

He remembered when he'd first met her three months ago at the psychiatrists' convention in New Orleans. He'd been overwhelmed by her. Bernstein had never kidded himself that he had any sort of sex appeal . . . after all, he was in his late thirties, he wasn't especially tall, he wasn't especially handsome, he wasn't especially anything . . . until Lana had completely captivated him. What had started off as a pleasant if somewhat cut-and-dried convention had turned into an erotic weekend beyond imagining.

He would have lied, cheated, given up everything for another taste of that. So when Lana had asked him to, upon returning to his native Malibu, seek out and take on a particular young woman's case, and suggested certain directions his consultations might take, Bernstein had been more than willing to do it. Somewhere in the back of his mind he had known he was being manipulated for some end he didn't understand. But he didn't care. He simply didn't care. His days were filled with thoughts of her, his nights with sensuous dreams.

"That was a naughty thing you did, Wong," she said scoldingly, her finger tracing lazy circles in the pillow. "Calling from the airport and saying you were already here. I hate having guests just pop up like this."

"Guest?" Bernstein was having trouble concentrating, the intoxicating aroma of her perfume wafting its way across the room to him. "I'd . . . I'd like to think I'm a bit more than a guest. God, it's good to see you, Lana. I . . ."—he took a step toward her—"I haven't been able to think of anything besides you. I had to see you again."

"Well," said Lana with a smile, "you didn't give

me much choice. I hope arranging to meet in this motel didn't inconvenience you."

He looked around, still not able to make out much of the room's contents and somehow pleased he couldn't. "To be honest, it's not terribly romantic," he said. "And I wish it were air-conditioned."

"Don't worry, Wong. There won't be any need for air conditioning, because we'll be heating things up in here."

He felt a tremor of excitement go through him. He dropped his carry-on bag and took a step toward her but halted in his tracks as she put up a hand. "First," she said, "tell me why you came all the way down here to Louisiana from California. What was so urgent that you couldn't simply telephone me, or drop me a line? Is it about—?"

"Abigail, yes." He nodded excitedly. "It's taken me a month of meeting with her almost every day, but I've convinced her she will never be able to put her own turmoil behind her unless she reconciles with her stepfather."

Lana sat up slowly, allowing one shoulder strap of her nightgown to drop alluringly down her arm. "You're quite certain she's going to act on this?"

"Absolutely. She trusts me implicitly. And it's good advice, really," he added, as much to convince himself as her. "My belief is before the month is out, Abigail Arcane will be coming down here to meet with your employer and put old demons to rest."

Lana said something under her breath Bernstein could have sworn was "Or create new ones." "What did you say?" he asked.

"Nothing, my love," said Lana, leaning back and stretching her arms out to him. "You've done wonderfully. My employer will be thrilled."

"It's . . . not your employer I was most concerned about," said Bernstein, becoming aware of his own pulse pounding against his temple as he walked toward her. "I was hoping . . . you might be grateful. That's why I came down. That's why—"

"And you were right, my love," said Lana. "So very right. Let me show you just how grateful I am."

He was across the remainder of the room in a flash, leaping onto the bed on top of her supine body, the mattress creaking noisily under him. He moaned as he felt her hands undoing the top of his slacks and sliding them down. "Oh, God, Lana," he moaned.

And the moment his buttocks were exposed she said softly, "Now."

"Now?" he gasped.

"Not you," she replied, and there was something in her eyes . . . as if she had just swallowed a helpless mouse.

Just at the edge of his peripheral vision something had separated from the shadows in the room and then, before his mind could fully register that something was wrong, terribly wrong, he felt a sharp stabbing pain in his right buttock.

He shrieked and rolled off her, hitting the floor

with a resounding thud, and he flopped around like a just-hooked fish. He tried to pull his trousers back up, but his arms refused to move. They simply lay there, two mutinous sacks of flesh and bone.

He looked up and someone was stepping back from him, an innocuous-appearing man with a high forehead, thinning hair, and a mustache. In his right hand he was holding a hypodermic . . . the hypo, Bernstein realized, that had moments before been injecting something into him.

Lana was standing next to him now, pulling on a robe over her nightgown. "How long will he be unconscious, Rochelle?"

The man she had called Rochelle said briskly, "At least an hour. More than enough time to get back to the compound." He leaned forward, waving a finger past Bernstein's eyes. "He's still awake. A strong specimen. We can use him."

"L-L-Lana . . ." Bernstein managed to get out.

Lana smiled down at him. "Yes, my love?"

"P-please . . . let me go . . ." He could barely hear his own voice, but clearly Lana had made out what he said.

She smiled and stroked his cheek, but there was no love to it now, only a clinical coldness. "Let you go? Wong, if you hadn't come down here, you wouldn't have put yourself in this position. Especially now when we needed subjects. Still . . . perhaps after Dr. Rochelle here is through with you, perhaps we will let you go. For old times' sake."

"I . . ." He licked his lips desperately, becoming aware of a fly, perched on the edge of the lamp. It wasn't flying, merely watching him. Anticipating. Waiting. "I won't tell anyone . . ."

"Of course you won't," said Lana. "When Dr. Rochelle is through with his experimenting, you certainly won't be in any condition to tell anyone anything."

"You . . . you bloodsucking bitch . . ."

Lana's hand lashed out and slapped him across the face. He took a dim measure of comfort in that he didn't feel it.

She stared at him with cold satisfaction and said, "Tell me, Dr. Rochelle . . . what was your next subject for the gene-splicing plan?"

"Well," said Rochelle, thoughtfully stroking his mustache, "I had been considering the *Hirudo medicinalis.*"

"And that would be . . . ?"

"The leech."

"Ah! How splendid. Dear, dear Wong Sing . . ." —she smiled down at him mirthfully—"you're going to find out about bloodsuckers firsthand."

What she was saying . . . this talk of gene splicing, of leeches, of—it wasn't possible. It was an insane, waking nightmare. She wouldn't. They couldn't—

And as if she were reading his mind, she said, "I would. They could. We will."

Somewhere from within him he found the last bit of strength he needed.

He screamed.

It carried high and long, hanging over the still air of the swamp. Alligators paused momentarily in their swimming; birds looked up but did not chirp. The echo of the scream hung there long after the source had lost the ability to utter a sound.

From his desk in the lobby, Alan looked up from the magazine he was reading. He paused and then slowly shook his shaggy, black-maned head.

"I told him he shouldn't have come here," he said, and then went back to his article.

Something . . . was trying to get . . . my attention.

The fly . . . saw a thousand images . . . of suffering . . . but it was only . . . human suffering . . . not the green.

I do not . . . care for humans. There is too much pain . . . in humanity.

Too much . . . hurt.

My consciousness . . . stirs slightly . . . and a few trees . . . rustle their branches . . . but then I return . . . to the peace . . . of the green.

I hope there are . . . no further disturbances . . . or I may have to . . . investigate.

2

Eunice Berger, a saleslady at Abby's New Wave Flower Shop, sat in the back office engrossed in watching a six-inch black-and-white image of Geraldo Rivera, his nose pleasingly bandaged, grilling an educator who claimed that watching *The New Adventures of Mighty Mouse* led to hard drugs. A well-read copy of *Roots* leaned against the set.

She half rose out of her seat when she heard the jingle of the bell hanging on the front door, indicating someone had entered, but when a cheery voice chimed out "Hi-ho, Eunice," she dropped back down.

Eunice, heavyset and bespectacled, was on a yogurt diet. She had created it herself. She reasoned that one cup of yogurt was slimming, so she was currently in the middle of her fifth cup of yogurt this morning (in the belief that that would be five times as good for her).

To say Abigail Arcane walked into the cramped

back office would be like saying a hurricane stirred up a little dust. Abby did not enter a room. She enveloped it.

A stunning young blonde, Abby somehow came across like a cheerleader for caffeine. Eunice was of the opinion that Abby had two modes: talk and sleep. Knowing Abby, she probably talked in her sleep as well. Of course, Eunice also knew that if she had half of Abby's looks, she'd have twice the social life she did.

If it had been the sixties, Abby would have been the quintessential flower child: this being the eighties, however, it was more stylish to think of her as the quintessential "flake." This was because her main concerns were with things that "real" people didn't worry about. The air. Plants. Water. Natural foods. Environmental action. Endangered animals. Far easier to think of Abby as a flake than to dwell on mankind's environmental shortsightedness. "Real" people had other priorities . . . like antiperspirants and automobiles.

In her midtwenties, Abby had the kind of figure that made construction workers choke on their whistles. At the moment that figure was clothed in a bizarre striped and flowered skirt-and-leg-warmers combination that looked as if it had been swiped from the wardrobe of *Godspell.*

"Great morning, Eunice!" she called. "Isn't it great?!"

Eunice didn't even answer the "Isn't it great" comment. With Abby it was always safe to assume any question posed was rhetorical. She turned back to the set as Abby began to speak to, and water, the assorted plants dotting their cramped office. They had name tags reading MURRAY, TOMMY, CHUCKY, and ANETTE.

"Morning, guys," she said, sounding distinctly chipmunkish. "This shrink I'm seeing, Wong Sing Bernstein, a shrink acupressure guy, right?" She turned to the next plant, splattering water from her watering can. "Guess what he says to me. None of my relationships will ever work until I confront my feelings about my stepfather. You know therapists. Everything's always related to families and stuff. Like there's not enough in the world to drive you nuts—you need relatives to really send you over the edge. Of course . . ."—she paused—"if Dr. Bernstein knew who I was talking to, I'd really be committed."

She bustled out into the main part of the shop and started chattering away at the other plants as she tended to their needs. At one point a potential client looked in through the window, but once he saw a cheery blond lunatic blathering at the begonias, it seemed a good cue to take business elsewhere.

"Why can't men be more like plants?" Abby said. "You can be nice to plants without them getting the wrong idea. Plants don't tell you they love you, then go back to their old girlfriends. Whoever heard of a plant doing anything mean or nasty? So what do you think?"

Eunice, in the office, heard with one ear that Abby was pausing, and thought it amusing that only Abby would wait for a reply from a nonhuman source.

Abby stared eye-to-eye with a sunflower. "I wish you wouldn't look at me that way."

She put down the watering can and stared out the window. She saw her reflection staring back at her, and in this light the ghostly image, in its very unreality, reminded her of the phantomlike recollections of another woman—someone who was beginning to slip away completely into the dimmest recesses of her memory.

Abby turned away then, but the image stayed with her. She pursed her lips and then looked back at the sunflower.

"Okay," she said softly, partially to the flower, partially to that ghost of another woman, "you're right. I'll do it. I'm not even going to call. I'm just going to go down there and confront him." She stood and continued her monologue as she walked toward the back office. "Why should he mess up my life? He sure didn't care about my mother. He didn't even give her a funeral . . . or if he did, he didn't invite *me*."

She strode into the back office and turned toward Eunice. She plunked the watering can down as if to emphasize her words as she said, "Eunice, I've got to go straighten out my life."

"Hallelujah!" Eunice erupted. "Girl, you are the most screwed-up person I know, and if you, of all people, have actually decided to get your shit together, then there is hope for the future of all humankind."

Actually, that was what Eunice intended to say. All Eunice managed to get out was "Ha—" before the good ship *Abigail* sailed right through her half of the conversation.

"I know you don't know what I'm talking about," said Abby, "but there's something I've got to take care of, and I can't do it by vegetating here in this store," and suddenly realizing her poor choice of words, she turned to the plants and said "Sorry about that" before turning back to Eunice and continuing, without taking a breath, "I'm going to see my hermit stepfather."

"That lunatic!" blurted out Eunice. "After ten years of telling me what a creep that guy is, how he's dangerous, how he should be turned into mulch, now you're going down into his backyard. Honey, if that's getting your life together, better you should stay disassembled."

Actually, that's what Eunice intended to say. This time she got as far as "That lu—" before Abby jumped in yet again.

"No, don't try to talk me out of it. Now, I'm leaving you in charge of my friends," and she waved at the plants. "I don't know when I'll be back."

"You're just waltzing off, just like that? That's not fair! You can't just vanish and leave me short handed without at least warning me."

Naturally that's what Eunice intended to say. This time she didn't even bother to open her mouth. She just stared at the TV.

"I'll call as soon as I can," said Abby as she

pulled on her wrap. "Keep them watered! And talk to them. They like you." She paused and then, bending over, shouted in Eunice's ear. *"Talk to them!* Here." She handed Eunice the watering can. "Leave the TV on. They love the Mets. And that cop who used to be in space, *T. J.* what's-his-name." She caressed the plants lovingly and said, "Good-bye, babies."

She barreled out of the store, and Eunice settled back to watch the rest of Geraldo and to enjoy the peace and quiet.

She would never see Abby again.

3

Think of the swamp as if it is a body. Its lungs provided by the great, lush trees and sinewy vines stretching around and through the system. Its heart and mind are deep within the green, the moist loam and dirt, teeming with thousands of microorganisms. Its blood is the water, water filled with life, water thick and cold yet somehow with an undercurrent of throbbing heat.

The lungs. The heart and mind. The blood.

Five foreign organisms had now entered the blood, and it coagulated around them, inspecting them, probing them. . . .

The five invaders had names: Harry Dugan, Bob Bissette, Morty Totleben, Chuck Veitch, and Dave Wrightson. Back in the office, in the safe, clean treasury department office, they had even had individual characteristics. Bob was tall and muscular, the immediate supervisor with sleeves usually rolled up, tie loosened, who started off each day with the exact same words: "It's show time." Harry, his second-in-command, was his physical opposite—shorter, thin, and bespectacled, zealously addicted to his two cups of morning coffee.

Morty was the department's best agent, and also the office rake. Word had gotten around about him, yet somehow there always seemed to be a new notch on his gun. Chuck, balding and thin, was the clock-watcher, rarely doing more than he had to but doing what he did with precise efficiency. Dave considered himself to be intellectually the superior of the group, and always wore a vest in the office since he said it indicated sincerity (and, as George Burns had said of acting, once you can fake sincerity, you got it made). He rarely, if ever, spoke, preferring to communicate his thoughts with withering glances.

Each of them had been individuals then, each with his own look and style, hopes and goals. But here, knee-deep in the blood of the swamp, they combined into one formless invading mass. All of them wore heavy, camouflage hunters' outfits, hats pulled down low around their ears (except for Morty's rather cheery fisherman's cap, which was perched jauntily to one side).

Wading through the blood, you lost your distinctiveness. You lost your uniqueness. If you weren't careful, you also lost your life.

It had seemed like such a good plan last Wednesday during their weekly poker game. Life was slow in the New Orleans office. All of them were dissatisfied with the pace of their individual careers. They needed to do something that showed initiative, that showed imagination, and that would let them kick some ass while they were at it to make up for the day-on-unending-day of involvement in two-bit operations.

The TV had been tuned in in the background to some old film they were barely paying attention to. Something about hillbillies or somesuch, and then all of a sudden shooting started in the program. They turned as one to watch as the hillbilly patriarch started shouting "Revenooers! Thar after the still! Run!"

The five drinking buddies had looked at one another then and grinned. "We're 'revenooers,' " Bob had said, in what can easily be classified as "famous last words."

"I think it's time to get out of the office and into the field," said Harry. "Y'know . . . there's a still somewhere in Suicide Swamp we've never been able to find. Two hick morons, Clyde and Gurdell, run it. Love to nail their asses."

And so Operation "Nail Their Asses" had been thrown into motion. A week later, armed with their courage, their wits, M16s, and six-packs of Coors back in the Land-Rover, the five "revenooers" had entered the bloodstream of the swamp with great expectations and visions of promotions.

Fifteen minutes into the expedition the disenchantment had set in.

The only sounds to be heard were the ones they themselves made. They slogged through the brackish water, the slime welcoming them to a place that was undoubtedly the rough draft for hell.

They stopped to get their bearings, swinging their powerful flashlights around and lighting on nothing except their own squinting faces, which were already covered with dirt and grim. Dave wiped an arm across his face in a vain attempt to clean it off and only managed to rearrange the filth that was already there.

Harry looked down nervously at the water that was waist deep on him. His high rubber boots were doing him not a bit of good as he felt the soggy mud beginning to accumulate around his feet. He wrinkled his nose in disgust.

At the head of the group, Bob gestured and pointed, and the others saw he was indicating a small mossy island just ahead of them in the bog. It seemed a comparative oasis in a desert of bilge.

They made for it, hopes buoyed by the thought of getting out of this garbage for even a few minutes. One by one they clambered up onto the island. Harry was the last one up, but as he tried to climb up he lost his footing and fell backward into the muck.

"Damn!" he snarled. "Damn damn damn!"

He tried to haul himself up but succeeded only in getting himself wetter. The other men glanced at one another, trying to decide whether they should do the humane thing and help him out, or enjoy a few more moments of amusement at his expense.

While they were deciding, Harry continued to rant, "Bugs! Snakes, 'gators. I hate this place! I'm tired of this slimy crap!"

As one, the men decided on the latter course of action and snickered at Harry's frustration. Trying to get his footing, Harry grumbled, "Go ahead, guys . . . yuk it up."

Taking pity on his second-in-command, Bob extended a hand. "Here," he said. "Grab hold and stop your griping."

Feeling more grateful than he wanted to show, Harry took it and staggered onto the comparative safety of the island. "Sheez . . . how the hell can I be so hot and cold at the same time?"

"Schizoid metabolism?" offered Morty.

Harry snorted at the lame attempt at humor while Bob managed to fish out Harry's glasses and started to wipe them off. "Whose idea was this, anyway?" Harry demanded.

"If memory serves," replied Bob, holding the glasses up to the small amount of moonlight available, "I think it was you who said, and I quote, 'I think it's time to get out of the office and into the field.' End quote."

"I said that?"

Bob replaced Harry's glasses on his face and patted his cheek. "Well, welcome to the field. Now, playtime's over. Let's find that still. Morty, take the point."

Reluctantly Morty complied and stepped back into the water, muttering "Why me?"

Bob followed directly behind him, followed by

Chuck, Dave, and Harry, to whom Dave turned and said tersely, "This time take up the rear instead of falling on yours."

Harry grimaced and, ignoring the exchange, Chuck said in a voice he thought was too soft for Bob to hear, "Take the point? Where does he get this crap?"

In the silence of the swamp, however, his voice carried, and Bob replied without looking, "Too many John Wayne flicks."

Harry paused only a moment to catch his breath, and that was when he heard a splash behind him. He wasn't sure where it had come from. It seemed to echo and re-echo all around him. He swung his flashlight around quickly, trying to discern where it had originated. His M16 was cocked and ready.

Nothing. The black mass of water seemed to suck the light in greedily, giving back no indication of what might lie beneath its surface.

He played the flashlight about a bit longer, then turned and headed toward his friends, who seemed intent on leaving him behind.

"Hey, guys," he called. "Guys!"

The moment he had turned away, the swamp's blood bubbled.

An Antibody rose slowly, peering through mad eyes at the departing mass of invaders.

The blood. Blood so thick with life, blood as red as the gleaming eyes of the Antibody.

The Antibody sank back into the blood as

Harry's voice could be heard in the distance, shouting "Wait up, guys!"

There is . . . something in the swamp . . . something human . . . followed by something . . . inhuman.

The inhuman . . . has thoughts and emotions . . . laid bare and evil. It will kill the humans.

But that is of . . . no concern to me. The bodies of the humans . . . will merely serve . . . to feed the swamp . . . and I am . . . the swamp . . . so why . . . should it matter.

The five men stopped short of the chain-link fence barring their progress. At first there was the brief hope that perhaps this was a fence created by the still owners, but Bob's flashlight played across a sign miraculously devoid of the muck that seemed to grow on anything that stood still for more than thirty seconds in the swamp.

The sign read: ARCANE CORPORATION. NO TRESPASSING.

An old line from a cartoon flittered through Harry's mind, Bugs Bunny's voice saying "I knew I shoulda made that right toin at Albequerque."

"Something tells me," Morty said slowly, "we're not gonna find that still around here."

Harry spoke up. "I told you we *(shoulda made that right toin at Albequerque)* took a wrong turn at that last bog."

Bob turned his light on his map. Naturally the still wasn't marked on it, and it wasn't even a hundred percent accurate as a guide, but he had thought it enough to keep them from getting lost. So, okay. He'd thought wrong. Just because they worked for the federal government, didn't mean they had to make a federal case out of it. "Can it, Dugan," he said in irritation to Harry. "I thought for sure we were headed in the right direction."

"You thought!" Chuck now said. "You stupid . . . if you could think, we wouldn't be here."

Bob shot him a glance indicating jobs were on the line, but he realized in the dimness Chuck couldn't see it, and besides, it seemed as if they had been wandering about in this mass for hours. It was natural for Chuck to be getting high-strung. "Take it easy, Chuck," he said, trying to sound mollifying.

But Chuck wasn't interested in being mollified. "No! Why couldn't we nab these moonshiners during the day, huh?"

"Because," said Bob, fighting to maintain his patience, "at night we have the element of surprise."

"Surprise!? We gotta find 'em before we can surprise 'em!"

Angrily Chuck grabbed the map out of Bob's hand and hurled it into the darkness behind them.

If they'd been listening, they would have heard the map bounce off something before hitting the water.

Something large and massive. Something inhuman.

• • •

The blood. The blood was so close now.

The Antibody moved through the swampblood toward the source of the infection now. It heard words being spoken, words that once upon a time would have made sense. Now, though, they were no more understandable than the buzz of the mosquitoes had been, back when the mosquitoes still buzzed. Back when there was noise in the swamp, instead of the silence that hung over it these dark days.

Harry stepped in quickly. This couldn't be allowed to progress. Chuck was getting married next month, for one thing . . . it wouldn't do for him to be unemployed when that happened. Especially since this would be his second wife, and he was still paying alimony to the first. "Gentlemen, gentlemen," he said placatingly. "you wanna kick the crap outta one another, fine. But do it back at the office."

The thought occurred to both men that back at the office they didn't want to fight since there was no point, and right after that they realized there was even less point to fight now. Especially since if one of them happened to knock out the other, all that meant was somebody was going to have to haul an unconscious body through the swamp. Who needed that?

"Hey, suits me," said Chuck.

"Fine," replied Bob, grateful to Harry for the interruption, and making a mental note to thank him when they got back to the office. "Then let's get back to the truck."

"Great," said Harry, genuinely glad to leave this place behind.

Bob consulted his compass and gestured in the direction of what he hoped was where the Land-Rover had been left. They started off after him . . . all except Morty, who hung back. Harry, accustomed to taking up the rear by this time, was surprised to be walking past Morty. "You comin', Mort?"

Morty, who had consumed the most beers on the way over, now felt a pressing need to rid himself of them. He turned toward a tree, his hand reaching for his fly as he said, "In a minute." He waited for Harry to take the hint, but Harry, who wasn't good on nonverbal cues, just stood there. Gesturing toward his crotch, Morty said, "Do you mind?"

Turning slightly red, and annoyed with himself that he hadn't realized right off the bat what Morty was talking about, he turned and headed off after the others.

Now, thought the Antibody. Now was the time. The infection was preparing to leave the swampblood, and that could not be allowed. The infection had to be punished for entering the bloodstream in the first place.

The infection had to give its blood to the swampblood, and to the swampblood's rightful denizen . . . the Antibody.

• • •

Morty finished up his last living act, turned toward his friends, who were departing in the distance, and suddenly felt a tug at his leg.

"What the . . ." he managed to say before he was suddenly yanked off his feet.

Before he could get out another word he was beneath the surface, the thick coagulating mass of water surrounding him, filling his lungs, choking him off. Something was still yanking at his leg. *'Gator!* came the frantic thought.

He should have been so lucky. . . .

Something human . . . has just died. It should not bother me . . . for death is a constant . . . in the swamp . . . and is a part of life . . . so this should be . . . of no consequence.

Why . . . then . . . is it . . . ?

Harry spun, hearing the abortive cry, the commotion and splashing behind him. This was not his imagination running overtime. Something was wrong. His flashlight swung out in the direction where Morty had been, and if the light caught Morty with something embarrassing hanging out, then so be it. Better embarrassment than . . .

Nothing. The powerful light couldn't detect a thing. There was the tree Morty had been standing in front of, but no Morty. "Morty? Mort?" he called out, and then louder, "Mort!"

Now the others had run up as Harry's alarmed

voice had gotten louder. "What's up?" demanded Bob. "What's all the yelling?"

"Morty's gone."

"What do you mean, gone?"

Harry was starting to lose it. It wasn't supposed to have gone this way. This was supposed to be a fun, macho, hoo-hah action kind of thing. Not a living nightmare, ass-deep in muck and friends vanishing. "I mean gone! One moment he was takin' a whiz by the tree, the next second, zip, nothin', history!"

As if Morty had been on stage with spotlights following him, Harry shone the flashlight on where his friend had been. The water had been rippling but was now still.

" 'Gator?" whispered Dave.

"Blood, man," said Chuck. "If it's a 'gator, wouldn't there be blood or something? There's nothing, man!"

"Okay, okay," said Bob, "he's gotta be here, guys. Fan out. We'll find him." He raised his voice. "Morty! Morty!"

And slowly something rose to the surface.

It caught just at the edge of the field of light, and Dave swung his M16 around, ready to blast it. But Chuck put out a hand, warning him off, and slowly they realized what it was.

Morty's distinctive fisherman's cap, no longer jauntily perched on his head, floated there, a silent marker for a grave of watery muck.

"Guys," said Chuck softly, "I don't think he can hear us."

And as Chuck became preternaturally calm, now it was Bob who began to stammer. "We . . . we gotta . . . we better get outta here."

Chuck grabbed him by the arm. "Hey, listen, buddy, we're not leavin' without Morty! You clear on that?"

It exploded from beneath the water.

The Antibody had just feasted, draining all the virulent blood from one of the five infections. The blood pumped through its mutated, misshapen body, giving it strength and power. Since its escape from the place with the gleaming walls, it had lain beneath the water, in the swampblood, conserving what little strength it had and draining blood from whatever it could find—alligators, mostly.

But human blood—that was unlike the cold, unappetizing life fluids of reptiles. Human blood was hot and passionate. It had flowed eagerly from the infection into the Antibody, and the Antibody had just as eagerly lapped up every drop.

Now it had found the other four infections. Now it would leech the vital blood from them, too, and, perhaps in so doing, gain enough strength to return to the place of the cold walls. To find the woman whose face it couldn't quite recall. He would find her. He would take her blood and then bring it to the swampblood for offering.

All of this . . . as soon as he cleared up this infection. . . .

He reached out, grabbing the closest one.

Dave screamed as the creature lashed out with unbelievable quickness, snagging him by the front of his coat and dragging him toward its mouth—

Mouth! In the name of God, what mouth?! What the hell was it!

It had put on Morty's clothes, and it didn't have arms. Instead it had huge, misshapen appendages. Its head was a monstrosity, sculpted from a child's deepest nightmares and brought to hideous life. Huge and black, the rear of the skull hung to partway down its back, while its shaking and quivering maw dangled in front of its chest.

The maw wasn't for chewing, Dave realized in one hideous moment before his death. It was some sort of sucking appendage. He had a quick glimpse of something red and moist before the maw lashed out and affixed itself to his face with a nauseating plopping sound. Something gouged into his cheeks, burrowed through his open, screaming mouth, and down; something was attacking his eyes . . . and then he lost consciousness. His life followed suit seconds later.

My God, thought Harry, even as he brought his M16 up and around; it's like a giant leech, and then he fired. Someone, Bob or someone, was screaming that he might hit Dave, but Harry knew that was certainly the least of Dave's problems. The others must have come to the same conclusion because instants later the air was alive with gunfire as they pumped round after round through Dave, into the Leech.

Dave slumped, riddled with holes, and there was no blood. . . .

For long seconds time froze there, there in the swamp as death hung all about them. . . .

And there was no blood. . . .

Except for a small trickle running down the side of the Leech's maw.

Jesus Christ, Harry's mind screamed at him, it's sucking him dry!

The triggers clicked together, the sound of the empty chambers in the rifles like an executioner's ax falling.

There were visible bullet holes in the Leech, but it didn't seem to be affected by them. It went on with its ungodly meal, and Dave's skin . . . what was visible of it . . . took on a deathly pallor.

Harry wanted to charge forward, to rip Dave's body from the creature's grasp, but his body simply refused to obey the directions of his mind. That was because his body was not suicidal.

They slammed new ammo cartridges home and fired again. The Leech dropped Dave's bloodless corpse, letting it slide underwater to be nourishment for the swamp. Bullets peppered the creature's body, and it staggered under the assault, but only from the impact. Bullets passed through or stayed in, but either way it seemed of little consequence to the Leech.

The Leech crouched now, looking from one man to the other, as if trying to decide which one to feast on next. Behind it the back of Dave's jacket was briefly visible as the body bobbed to the surface for a moment before sinking down into the mire.

Once again they were out of ammo, and this time their collective nerve had vanished with the expenditure of the last shell.

"Let's get the hell out of here!" shrieked Harry.

"Good idea!" Chuck shouted back, and they bolted.

They plunged blindly through the swamp, not caring about one another, or even exactly where the truck was now. All they were concerned about was getting as far from the Leech creature as possible.

Chuck and Bob started to widen the gap between themselves and Harry, and then Harry tripped over something (*An arm! No, a sunken tree branch*), and by the time he had hauled himself up, his friends had disappeared into the darkness ahead. He wasn't sure which direction they had gone in, and his frantic shout of "Guys!" met with nothing more than deathly silence, broken only by the crashing of trees somewhere in front of him, his own ragged breathing, and splashing . . .

. . . behind him. . . .

It was coming after him, slowly, ponderously,

taking its time because he was lost and alone and more terrified than he had ever been.

He started to run again, trying not to think of Dave's lifeless eyes staring into the muck of the bottom where he was submerged, and of the worms and millions of microscopic creatures already beginning to devour him . . . and Morty, dear God, Morty, sucked dry, the lifeblood pouring into the ungodly mouth of some thing. . . .

He was certain he was heading toward the Land-Rover, that blessed truck that would be his salvation. . . .

Their friend and comrade completely forgotten, replaced by the overwhelming imperative to survive, Bob and Chuck shoved their way through the swamp. Water they would have carefully waded through before, they now plunged into headlong, certain that any moment the *thing* that had taken Morty and Dave would have them next.

Their earlier bickering was as beyond recall as was Harry. They had been prepared for belligerent hooch-makers, even angry 'gators. But this . . . this was beyond rational comprehension, and indeed insanity was knocking at the doors of their minds asking ever so politely to be allowed in.

And at that moment, magically, the undergrowth seemed to part, and they stood gasping on a dirt road. Bob felt a wave of retroactive nausea hit him, but he managed to push it back, just barely.

Then a motor was gunned from nearby, and instants later a Jeep with four heavily armed men burst out from the undergrowth. Like a well-trained platoon the men leapt out of the vehicle as it screeched to a halt.

For a crazed moment Bob thought they were reinforcements from the office, and he wondered who the hell had known they were coming out there. But then he realized they were wearing uniforms of some sort of private security force, and there was a curious insignia on them. Still, who cared? They were human; they were heavily armed; they were here. Big as life. Real. Not some creature from a drug-induced nightmare.

Between gasps Bob said, "Boy . . . are we ever glad . . . to see you guys."

The guards glanced at one another, saying nothing. Bob didn't think anything of their silence, assuming they were giving Chuck and him a moment to catch their breaths, but when he glanced up, he saw a rather sinister-looking pistol being aimed right at him.

Now Chuck noticed as well, and he stammered out "Hey . . . hey, look, wait a minute . . . we're government agents. . . . You can't just . . . just . . ."

The pistol spat out two silent shots, like metallic hiccups.

The Antibody would not have all the infections, it seemed. Two of them had slipped away, but there was still one ahead, running as fast as it could, but it would certainly not be fast enough. The Antibody felt charged with life thanks to the stolen blood coursing through it. Power and speed sang in its body, and it effortlessly followed the fleeing infection. Perhaps, after feeding on that one, it would manage to locate the other two. Perhaps not. Ultimately it didn't matter. The swampblood would be cleansed in any event, and only the cleansing and the blood mattered. Only the blood.

He should have been at the truck by this time, he was certain. Harry's abrupt realization that he had gotten turned around, that the truck was back in the creature's direction, caused him to try and skid to a halt, and his feet went out from under him. He tried to break his fall but didn't succeed. He hit the water and momentarily went under before he pulled himself up, splashing and coughing.

He reached up automatically to adjust his glasses and realized to his horror they weren't there. They had fallen off into the water.

Without them he was practically blind. Even if by some miracle he managed to find his way out of this murky nightmare and locate the truck, he wouldn't be able to drive more than fifty yards without running off the road. Why the *hell* hadn't he worn his contacts for this insane adventure?

He started scrambling around in the water, certain the Leech was closing in on him.

It was going to find him. Find him and kill him, sucking him dry. It was unreal, unnatural, an affront against God and humanity, but it was killing them all.

It couldn't be allowed to win. It was unfair, unjust, not possibly part of the grand scheme of things in creation.

There was, Harry thought, as he shoveled his way through the mire, searching for those damned plastic-and-glass, thirty-five-dollar bits of salvation, there was no God.

And in the distance he heard something splashing, a faint sucking sound as if a slippery-slick mouth was opening and closing in anticipation. It was coming his way.

No, God, he thought bitterly. Or if there was, then He was certainly not here in the swamp.

There it is . . . again.

The agony . . . and suffering . . . that seems to be . . . humanity's hallmark. Overwhelming now.

Two bodies . . . are already decomposing . . . in my waters. I feel them . . . becoming assimilated and . . . a part of me . . . and I feel . . .

Something unnatural . . . something wrong. The bodies . . . are not right . . . and now I sense . . . another presence . . . in the swamp . . . something not of the swamp . . . not of the green . . . not of the earth.

There are too many . . . disturbances . . . disrupting my rest. There is no peace . . . in the green this night.

I must . . . investigate.

I reach out . . . with the tendrils of . . . my consciousness . . . and feel the swamp . . . breathing around me . . . the womb . . . moist and cool and loving . . . that harbors me. I must . . . leave the womb . . . if I am ever to have peace . . . once more.

But I will need . . . a body.

Once . . . I had a body . . . like that of a human. Now how did it go . . . ?

Yes . . . though the memory pains me . . . I begin to recall.

I must . . . mold the green . . . as best as my hazed recollection . . . can do.

I begin to rise . . . from the darkness . . . passing the worms and ants . . . passing the hidden places . . . that are not hidden from me . . . up to the surface . . . of the swamp. I sense . . . rather than see . . . the moon hanging in the sky . . . a great glowing eye . . . watching to see what happens . . . this night.

I am . . . in the grass . . . in the weeds . . . in the vine . . . in the dirt. I am in them . . . and of them.

Yes . . . a body . . . to leave the womb.

The head will be first . . . followed by shoulders. I pull all the green . . . growing things of the swamp . . . to me . . . fashion a head . . . and I see for the first time . . . in a long time . . . the world around me . . . through vaguely human eyes . . . the way humans . . . saw the world around them . . . when they first rose . . . from the primordial muck. How would it have been . . . I wonder . . . had the muck risen with them . . . ?

I reach out . . . and find the thickest dirt . . . the sturdiest branches . . . the strongest vines. I have unclear recollections . . . of organs that are needed . . . lungs, kidneys. I have need . . . of an anatomy lesson . . . but I sense there is . . . little time . . .

To be safe . . . I fashion organs . . . from plant fiber . . . and position them . . . where I think they should be. My head and shoulders . . . are now fully formed . . . and I begin to create . . . a skeletal mass of bark . . . and woodstuffs . . . and cloak it . . . in a skin of weed and lichen . . . wet, slick, and pulsing . . . with the life of the earth . . . of the green.

All around me now . . . are popping sounds . . . as slick vines intertwine . . . leaves slap against one another. I create a circulatory system . . . of hollow vines and tubers . . . and pump into it . . . the water of the swamp . . . the lifeblood . . . of my world.

I raise my arms . . . massive and strong . . . as strong as the earth . . . and I hear a rustling . . . and realize it is me.

Part of me . . . is aware . . . this body is not human. It is not meant to be . . . but merely an approximation . . . in honor . . . of a rebirth.

I look down . . . and see my feet . . . are rooted to the ground. The earth mother . . . does not wish to part with me . . . but I must probe the mystery . . . of what is happening in the swamp.

I lift my right leg . . . and with a snapping sound . . . the roots rip free . . . and moments later the left . . . and the earth mother . . . with a sob . . . releases me. I shamble forward . . . the living embodiment . . . of nature . . . seeking out what is unnatural.

And I remember . . . that the newly born cry.

I tilt my head back . . . run a tongue of vegetable matter . . . across teeth of wood . . . and howl a greeting.

4

The alligators knew.

The water birds knew.

The small, furry creatures and the larger, cold-blooded creatures shared as one in the knowledge.

And more . . .

At the Wein Motel, Alan the desk clerk was doing the London *Times* crossword puzzle when he swatted away a fly buzzing in his ear.

That was when he realized. He looked up, watching the fly circle the room lazily, and it was buzzing—the damned thing was making a noise.

"Oh, tell me it's so," he could barely whisper.

And then, from deep within the swamp, a cry wafted through the air. A cry as new as an infant, as old as the earth.

Alan smiled through his thick beard and said, "So . . . you've returned. About bloody time."

• • •

Harry felt around frantically, certain any second he would manage to lay his hands on his glasses. Certain he would be able to regain control of this nightmarish situation.

His questing hands reached out and grasped something hard: a misshapen leg.

He knew immediately what it was, and he threw himself backward frantically, his heart sinking. The Leech reached down and hauled him to his feet.

He felt the Leech's fetid breath blast into his face, and he struggled fiercely, his throat paralyzed with fear. Then he found his voice and started to scream, locking his arms and legs against the Leech's chest in vain hope of accomplishing what two of his peers had already failed to do: live.

"Please, no!" As the sucker prepared to close on his face, Harry sent out a plea to the entity he was certain had deserted him. "Oh, God, please!"

And suddenly he was torn, as if by divine force, from the grasp of the Leech. He had a brief impression of leaves, of sinewy muscle as strong as a tree, and then he was hurled backward, tumbling end over end.

He never thought he would be so happy to land in the thick, unpleasant water of the swamp. But at least he was alive to do it.

He scrambled up out of the water, peered through the darkness and haze as best he could. His mind screamed at him to run, to get the hell out of there, not to question what had just happened but merely be thankful it had while quickly covering ground.

But he couldn't. He stared, anchored to the spot. Rooted. Trying to make out the bizarre scene playing out before him.

The Antibody hesitated. Its instinct told it something had just prevented it from destroying the infection. And that something was now standing before it, waiting, appraising. It watched the Antibody carefully through two small, glowing red eyes that seemed to float in huge pools of black.

Dimly the notion began to fight through to what served as the Leech's mind that this was no new intruder it faced now. This was not another invasion of the bloodstream. This . . . this *was* the bloodstream. This was the heart of the swamp, the brain of the swamp now sending new instructions to the Antibody.

The heart and brain of the swamp pointed.

The order was clear. Leave the body.

The Antibody was staggered. It was part of the body now. It had no humanity left, so it had to be part of the swamp. If the swamp rejected it, it had nothing.

Perhaps . . . perhaps it had always had nothing. Perhaps the idea that it was a defender against invasion was a delusion. Yes, yes, it was becoming clear. It was not an Antibody. It was just . . . just a parasite. A bloodsucking leech, a monster with no purpose except to destroy, to feed off the living.

The living swamp was still pointing, still ready to banish the Leech.

The unnatural, banished by nature. The unreal, forced to face reality. It was too much. Too much for the Antibody. Too much for anybody.

Harry watched in horror as the Leech went berserk.

He could barely make out the Leech's opponent: He was tall and dark, filthy as hell and covered with vines and leaves, and smelling of dirt. And then, with a scream torn from an inhuman throat, the Leech leapt at him, that terrible sucker mouth lashing out and clamping down onto the face of the newcomer.

Harry gasped and, in defiance of all logic, actually got a little closer. For the Leech was having trouble with the newcomer. This . . . this swamp man stood there with incredible patience while the Leech was trying to find some sort of a hold on him. It was tough going. Huge pieces of dirt and weed came off in the Leech's hand. Its sucker mouth pulled away clumps of mud, desperately seeking somewhere on that impassive face to latch onto.

Then the swamp man reached out and, as if dealing with a child, lifted the Leech man high over his head. He half twisted and hurled the monstrosity a dozen yards, the Leech smashing into a large tree. The Leech slid down to the ground, momentarily stunned, and the swamp man splashed through the water toward it, silent and pulsing with power.

The Leech stood, turned, and uprooted the tree.

Of all things, ripping the tree from the ground seemed to stagger the swamp man for a moment. He looked disoriented, as if the act of the separation had actually been felt by him. The Leech, seizing upon whatever opportunity it could, charged forward, slamming the tree around like a battering ram. It caught the swamp man midsection, knocking him down into the water.

Harry could feel the impact all the way from where he was standing. Whoever was fighting the Leech, he had to be dead or dying from that blow. Crushed ribs, punctured lungs, could be the only results from such a pounding.

The Leech advanced on the swamp man and slammed the tree down, pinning the swamp man beneath it. "Get away from him!" screamed Harry, but if the Leech heard, it paid no mind. The swamp man struggled clumsily, as if unused to his own body, and he placed one arm against the tree and tried to lever it off.

Immediately the Leech perched on top of the tree, finding tentative traction on the slippery branches, and it grabbed the swamp man's arm and pulled, pulled with all its strength, all its madness. . . .

It ripped the arm from the swamp man's socket with a horrible *splutch* sound.

Harry sank to his knees, now waist-deep in the

water, moaning in fear and illness. That was that. Now blood would fountain from the amputated arm, from the maimed shoulder, and the Leech would drink deep, become stronger still, and they were going to die.

But there was no blood.

Even without his glasses, Harry could see there was no blood. But the swamp man was still alive. How could it be?

Not only was he still alive, but now he was fighting back.

Harry had once been in lumberjack territory some years ago, and had heard the cracking sound of a tree as it was falling over, the moan of something hundreds of years old protesting its fate.

He heard that roar now, impossibly, from the throat of the swamp man: the roar of the wood as the swamp man hurled the tree, with the Leech creature on top of the tree, off himself using his legs and good arm.

The Leech leapt clear and advanced on the swamp man once gain. Meantime the swamp man was fishing beneath the water, apparently searching for the lost arm.

Yes, Harry was thinking insanely, find the arm. Pack it on ice. It can be saved, reattached. . . .

Just as the Leech got within range, the swamp man stood, holding the severed arm by the wrist. He turned and swung it at the Leech.

The arm smashed across the Leech's face, staggering the creature. The Leech tried to pull itself together, but another blow spun it completely around, and it fell into the water. It pulled itself up just in time to have the arm smash down on its back.

Calmly, implacably, the swamp man pounded on the Leech using his own severed arm. The Leech couldn't mount an offense, couldn't even get a defense going. The swamp man continued to batter it mercilessly, moving faster and faster as he became more confident, more powerful. The more of a beating the Leech took, the greater the swamp man's strength seemed to become.

Now the Leech looked as if it could barely stand, and the swamp man swung the arm again, caving in the side of the Leech's head. It sank beneath the water, and the swamp man advanced on where it had gone under, still clutching the arm and waving it threateningly.

Harry tried futilely to rub the dirt from his eyes, and then suddenly the swamp man turned and shambled toward Harry. Harry stood unmoving, too tired and too terrified to budge as the swamp man bore down on him.

Oh, God, I'm next, he thought.

The swamp man dropped his lopped-off arm, and his good hand lashed out toward Harry. Harry shrieked.

But the swamp man was reaching over Harry's head. Tentatively Harry looked up and saw the swamp man was now holding the head of a snake, which was snapping and hissing angrily at him.

Slowly Harry craned his neck around and saw the snake's long coils wrapped around the tree branch overhead. It was then it dawned on him: The snake had been about to strike, and the swamp man had ensured that hadn't happened.

Harry had been saved twice in one night. Not bad.

The swamp man pulled the snake down from its perch, turned, and hurled the reptile a fair distance away.

Harry looked down and almost started to scream again, for now a hand was reaching up at him from the bog, and he thought the Leech was trying to get him again. Then he realized, though, it was the hand, leaf-and-muck–encrusted, belonging to the rest of the swamp man's arm the Leech had torn off.

He pointed and managed to get out, "You . . . you better have that arm taken care of. . . . Maybe you can still . . . still . . ."

The swamp man looked down, picked up the now-useless arm. Harry was incredulous. He didn't consider himself squeamish, but he would have had real trouble even touching a dismembered portion of his own anatomy, much less pick it up and study it with the clinical detachment this guy had.

The swamp man turned the arm around and placed the upper arm against the shoulder.

Harry tried to see clearly, and indeed he was seeing what was happening but simply couldn't accept it.

Root and tendrils were shooting from the arm, and the shoulder was intertwining amid little sounds of *spuk* and *pwop* and *fwep.* At first the arm hung loosely, and then it was pulled tightly against the shoulder, the seam vanishing, the moss-encrusted muscles starting to flex.

It was as if the arm had never been detached. The swamp man bent it at the elbow, moved the fingers, and nodded his great head, satisfied.

Harry sat down hard in the water. Once such indignity would have elicited a symphony of complaints from him. Now Harry wasn't even aware of it.

He knew he owed this . . . creature . . . his life. That whatever he was facing was sure as hell more benevolent than the monster that had been chasing him, which had sucked his friends dry and been ready to do the same to him.

Thinking of the Leech, Harry cast a nervous glance in the direction where the monster had last gone under. There was no sign of it. It was either dead or, hopefully, mortally injured. Still, his major concern at the moment was what he was facing right now.

"You . . ." He licked his lips, spitting out the dirt his tongue found there. "You're not human?"

It was more or less a rhetorical question. Nevertheless the great creature before him slowly shook its head.

"What . . . are you?" asked Harry.

The creature paused, considered this. And then he spoke, his voice funereal, pulled from somewhere deep within himself, from deep within the earth. Each word was an effort, each syllable a challenge. But he spoke just the same.

"The swamp," he said.

" 'The swamp'?" Harry repeated in confusion. "The swamp isn't alive. It's just a . . . a thing."

He does not . . . understand. He would never say that . . . if he did understand . . . or ever could . . . but I will put it . . . in a way he may yet . . . understand. . . .

And he spoke one more time to Harry Dugan in his sepulchral voice.

"Yes . . . a thing . . . and I am . . . the Swamp Thing."

5

Alan the desk clerk heard the familiar muttered profanity, this time distinctly from a female voice, and he put down his magazine and called out, "Knob come off again?"

The door was pulled open as sunshine flooded into the musty interior of the lobby. Alan squinted, putting an arm up against the sun's brilliance, as an attractive blond woman, dressed far more appropriately for the shores of Malibu than the shores of Suicide Swamp, struggled in. She was hauling a small red checked bag and audibly grunting.

He imagined the bag hadn't seemed all that heavy when she'd started out on her odyssey. The humidity of the swamp, however, tended to take its toll. She dropped the bag and paused, waiting for her eyes to become accustomed to the dimness. She pulled in frustration at the tank top adhering to her skin since she had become covered with sweat.

"Got a phone here?" She addressed the general dark, still not quite certain where anything or anyone was.

Ordinarily Alan would have directed her to the pay phone around back, but something about her prompted him to take pity on her. He reached under the desk and pulled out a small unit and said, "Right here, love."

She walked over slowly, now clearly able to make out objects. In addition to the tank top she wore a pink miniskirt and stylish bright blue tights. She paused a moment and said, "Excuse me," then turned her back to him, slid out of her shoes, and with a quick movement, pulled down the tights.

"Nicely done," said Alan appraisingly.

"Thanks," she replied, wadded the tights into a sopping ball, and stuffed them into her bag. She withdrew a pair of thigh-high white stockings and pulled them on. Then she picked up the phone and stopped, her finger poised over the dial. "Who am I calling?" she asked.

"Couldn't say, love."

"Right. A taxi."

"Didn't you just get here in a taxi?" said Alan. "I could have sworn I heard one pull away just now."

"Yeah, well . . . he heard where I wanted to go and wouldn't take me there. Oh, he agreed to it when he picked me up at the airport, but his nerve ran out."

"Well . . ."—Alan steepled his fingers, leaning

on the edge of the desk—"where did you want to go?"

"The Arcane Mansion."

He looked at her askance, his hair covering his face so only his sunken eyes were visible. "Why would you want to go to that godforsaken place?"

"The guy who runs it is my stepfather. I'm Abigail Arcane."

He was silent for a long moment. "Condolences."

"What do you mean by—"

"Look, love," he said affably. "Why not check in to this place? Stay a night or two. Soak in the beautiful atmosphere. . . ."

"I'm soaking enough already."

"And then turn around and leave. I already gave that advice to one chap, and he didn't listen. Perhaps you might."

"Well, I'd really like to, but I can't put this off any longer. Now . . ."—she held the phone impatiently—"who should I call?"

He sighed and pushed a small advertisement for a taxi service. "You'll have to tip the chap a hefty bit, but they'll get you there."

She gave a quick nod of thanks and made the call as Alan stepped back, his arms folded. There was something about her, he realized, something he couldn't quite put a finger on.

She certainly didn't carry with her any of the pure evil that seemed to radiate from Casa Arcane. No, she seemed to have just the opposite about her.

"About twenty minutes? Fine, I'll be in the lobby," she said, then hung up. And now she was looking not at Alan, but just past him. "Excuse me," and she came around the desk and went straight to a potted fern that was positioned listlessly on the table behind him.

She started to murmur to the plant in low, encouraging tones. Alan watched her speculatively. "It seems to like you," he said at length.

"I've always gotten along real good with plants," she said.

"That's a knack that will serve you in good stead out here."

She turned and said thoughtfully, "You're British, aren't you?"

"That's right, love."

" 'Cause that's not the kind of accent I'd expect to hear in the middle of the bayou. What in the world are you doing around here?"

"Oh . . ."—he glanced around—"it reminds me of where I grew up."

"They have swamps in England?"

"Boggy areas, actually. That's where I hail from: the moor."

"Well, then . . ." She stopped, realizing she didn't know his name.

"Alan," he supplied helpfully.

"Well, then, Alan of the Moor, do you actually make a living out of this place? I saw a vacancy sign outside."

"At the moment we have only one guest," he

said, sounding almost apologetic, and he pointed. "That chap right there."

Abby turned and gasped, startled.

There was a man seated in a large wicker chair, tucked over in the shadows of the corner. He simply stared out, not appearing to focus on much of anything.

"Who's that?"

"Government chap. Harry something-or-other. Came out of the swamp a day or so ago, blithering, crying, barely coherent. Telling crazy stories about . . . well, I needn't bore you with them. Sheriff came by not too long ago and talked to him about it. Doing some further checking, but he doesn't expect to find much. The swamp is very skilled at keeping its secrets from almost everyone."

"Almost?"

"Well," and he came the closest he had to a smile since she'd arrived, "I know them all, of course."

"Why you?" she said, smiling back.

"Because at night, when the darkness calls to me . . . I answer back. And the darkness favors me with the secrets of the things it hides."

She stared at him. There was a look of mild dementia in his eyes.

"The darkness has spoken of you to me," he said.

"Oh . . . has it?" she replied, suddenly wishing she'd never set foot out of the flower shop.

"Yes. Oh, I didn't realize at first that it was

you. Merely someone like you. Someone who would be part of the tangled skein about to be uncoiled. There will be a great duel here, you see. You will be there for the beginning, and you will be there at its end. You are the humanity that will give strength to nature for its challenge."

"And you are a mental case," said Abby, backing up out the door. She paused and called out to Harry, "I'd get out of here if I were you!"

"Oh, he will . . . when he's ready," said Alan.

"Well, I hope he's good and ready soon, because he's going to be a complete basket case if he hangs around here listening to you spout off with your imaginary stories!"

Grabbing her bag at the last moment, Abby stepped out into the sunlight and went to the far end of the porch to wait for the cab.

"Of course they're imaginary stories," Alan called out, and grinned darkly. "Aren't they all?"

6

Sheriff Buford T. Beaumont, a classic "good ol' boy" who liked to claim he was the prototype for the sheriff in *Smokey and the Bandit,* slammed on his brakes. The police car skidded in the dirt as the young boy darted nimbly around the careening front fender.

He was a lanky, twelve-year-old black kid, with a borrowed thirty-five-millimeter camera hanging around his neck. Seeing the sheriff's irate expression, he grinned and snapped off a quick photograph.

"Omar Brown!" shouted Beaumont, shaking a beefy fist, "wait'll I tell your parents!"

"Ain't home!" replied Omar, and bolted off into the underbrush.

Beaumont grunted and backed up slowly, nervous that Omar's sidekick Darryl might be hanging around somewhere, and he'd probably allow himself to get run over.

Then he started forward again, and in the distance he could now make out the Arcane Mansion.

He hated the place.

It had been there since the Civil War, once an elegant mansion, a place of delicate manners and polite, studied courteousness. Even the evil of slavery had not detracted from the surface beauty of what had been.

Now, though, over a century later, the evil had erupted up from the earth and overtaken the manse. Now a chain-link fence surrounded the perimeter, and Beaumont was approaching the gate where two men in coveralls were standing guard.

Behind them, now an elegant canker, was the abode of Arcane.

There were many places night's cloak seemed to render singly inhospitable. Creatures appeared to hide in the shadows, eager and hungry and waiting for innocent passersby. In the harsh reality of daylight, however, such imaginings usually vanished, to be replaced by innocuous reality.

At the mansion of Anton Arcane, though, even at high noon the shadow creatures seemed to be there still.

Dr. Lana Zurrell, no longer in her seductive and destructive nightgown, but clad now in stern dress and no-nonsense lab coat, continued to process information into the hungry banks of the computer.

Whereas outside one could drown in the heat,

here in the underground lab it was refreshingly cool, even brisk. Carved out of rock and earth, the lab was a curious mixture of chrome and glistening cave stone. Masses of electronic machinery sat everywhere, bizarre additions to the nature of the rock.

When she had first come here, Zurrell had been spellbound. Now it held little interest for her . . . as little interest as did the handful of perpetual security guards who hovered nearby in loose groups.

She input the last of the data and sat back, rubbing her tired eyes. Then she felt a hand drop softly onto her shoulder.

Only one man in the compound would dare touch her. Indeed, he was by coincidence the same man who was actually capable of coming up behind her so softly, she had not been alerted by so much as a footfall.

"So?" The voice that came from behind her was low and sibilant, with a discernible French accent bespeaking his European upbringing.

She turned and stood to face him.

Arcane waited with studied patience, arms folded across his crisp white shirt. His straight black hair was tinged gray, his square-jawed face appearing carved from harsh granite.

"The two new patients," she told him, "are recovering from the operation. Dr. Rochelle has high hopes. The others . . ."

She stopped, unsure whether her words would anger him.

"Yes," he said in carefully modulated tones. "What about them?"

"Well . . ."—she sighed—"see for yourself."

Arcane and Zurrell walked over toward the "patients"—a bizarre collection of half-man, half-animal creatures penned in cages. Insanely they all wore cheerful blue hospital gowns.

They stood there, making frantic gestures, opening their mouths or beaks or snouts and screaming or shrieking or bellowing. They pounded on the glass, and they were the zoo of a madman's dreams.

But there was no sound. At most the glass shook slightly under the pounding of some of them, but that was all.

Arcane paused momentarily, then reached over and snapped a switch. Over a loudspeaker now came a nightmarish cacophony, and even Lana Zurrell, who had hardened herself to the grisly sights she witnessed, turned away.

Arcane smiled, drinking it in, before snapping off the sound and returning them to their mute state.

Lana tried to find someplace to gaze that would not sicken her. She found herself staring at an elephant. The elephant turned and, in profile, an agonized human face looked back at her.

She closed her eyes and, with effort, shook it off, pulling together her professional detachment and draping it over her like a shroud. "The gene splicing has gone extremely well. We're very close to hitting on the right DNA combination."

Raising a finger and waving it as if chiding a child, Arcane said, "I somehow sense that's an unfinished sentence . . . so finish it, please."

"Well . . . some of the rejected specimens have obviously mutated rather startlingly."

He raised his eyebrows in surprise and gestured at the creatures. "*Obviously* seems too mild a word. I am quite aware of the mistakes, Lana. Both the ones here . . ." he paused, "and the one that got away into the swamp. The Leech, I believe."

He said nothing further for a moment, and Lana thought, he knows! He knows I let Bernstein into the swamp! But I couldn't stand having him around here, knowing I let that . . . that thing into me, even if I did it for you, Anton; oh, God, don't punish me. . . ,

If Arcane knew how the Leech had escaped, he gave no indication. "What I'm interested in is results. How is Dr. Rochelle doing with the new ones?"

She gestured toward the door connecting into the lab.

They walked into the room where Rochelle was hunched over a gurney, oblivious as always of anything else going on.

Lana had heard of Dr. Newton Rochelle long before she'd met him. The "Doctor" was purely an honorary title now, since he'd been stripped of his right to practice medicine long years ago by the AMA because of his gruesome and inhumane experiments. His case had been notorious in medical annals; theories so loathsome, lab tests so heinous, that even the most stonyhearted researchers were sickened.

Since then he had dropped out of sight, and the medical profession had heaved a collective sigh of relief. If they could have seen what his current activities were, the medical profession would have been heaving something else.

Rochelle turned and started slightly when he saw Arcane. Arcane's pointed look of interest in the occupant of the table garnered a dismayed shrug from Rochelle.

On the table were the remains of Chuck, the former clock-watcher, for whom time had seemed to pass with a vengeance. If his fiancée could have seen him, which thank God she never would, she would not have recognized him. Rochelle had just been disconnecting the last of the tubes attached to his withered form. His face was old beyond comprehension, wrinkled and bloodless. He was bald, his eyes sunken and lifeless, his mouth toothless and his gums blackened.

"I'm afraid the genetic serum worked in reverse again on this one," said Rochelle apologetically. "Perhaps it was the tranquilizer darts your men used. Affected the blood . . ."

"Rochelle," said Arcane, now visibly holding his temper in check, "you've been at this for months. No significant developments. Only a zoo full of misshapen monstrosities and a cemetery's worth of corpses. I need the rejuvenation formula perfected."

"And we will have it," Lana said quickly.

"When?" snapped Arcane.

"Soon." She prompted Rochelle. "Won't we, Doctor?"

Rochelle was clearly unsure, but hastily he said, "Ah . . . yes. Quite soon, Dr. Arcane."

Momentarily satisfied, or at least pretending to be, Arcane moved off toward another operating table. On it was another recent example of Rochelle's handiwork.

Bob, also late of the treasury department, was strapped down. The good news was he was alive. The bad news was he was alive.

Arcane stared down at him impassively, watching Bob's mandibles click in horrified frustration. His segmented body twisted; his multiple legs clawed futilely at the air. Antennae protruded from what was once a human face.

"And what's that?" asked Arcane, his eyes narrowing.

"Another disappointment," said Rochelle, shaking his head. "Terrible. I tried mingling his genes with a member of the Blattidaean family. . . ."

"A what?"

"Cockroach," clarified Rochelle.

Arcane coughed politely. There was, of course, no reason for Rochelle to have performed such an abominable cross. He was clearly making use of Arcane's facilities to indulge his own ghoulish side interests, in the guise of trying to help Arcane with his own . . . difficulties.

Rochelle would definitely have to be brought into line. That, however, could wait. This . . . abomination . . . could not.

"We have enough insects in this place, Doctor," said Arcane, and momentarily Rochelle wondered if he himself was the insect being referred to. "Destroy it before it multiplies, please."

With a deferential nod, Rochelle turned the gurney around and wheeled it toward a large, glass-enclosed unit resembling a heavily wired telephone booth. He pulled the door open, then briskly unstrapped the thing that had once been Bob and lifted it off the table.

Lana shuddered at the sight of it. No matter how long she'd been around these things, she would never be able to bring herself to handle one of them so calmly.

Bob was surprisingly light, or perhaps not so surprisingly considering his entire skeletal structure had metamorphosed into something literally Kafkaesque. Rochelle coolly shoved Bob into the unit and closed the door, latching it from the outside.

"It's in the disposal unit, sir."

"I can see that," said Arcane. "Therefore, I would suggest you dispose of it."

Rochelle went to the side of the unit where there was a control panel with a simple on/off switch. The cockroach creature seemed to be trying to focus on him, clearly not understanding anything that was happening.

The moment Rochelle flicked the switch, the

unit began to hum. The high-pitched noise alarmed the creature terribly, and it began to pound on the door, its legs making hideous clacking and scratching noises. When this had no effect, it threw its brown crusted body against the side of the booth. The unit trembled slightly but gave no indication it was suffering any strain from the pounding.

Suddenly the cockroach creature was hit with searing blue arcs of electricity. For one brief moment it rediscovered its humanity as an all-too-human scream was ripped from its throat. It twisted, writhing in agony, and then flame erupted from between the joints of its segmented body. Desperately, uncomprehendingly, it tried to slap out the flames, and then the thing blew apart. The interior of the unit was now covered with burning shell, rapidly becoming ash, and the air was filled with the stench.

Rochelle calmly watched the entire execution, having had the foresight to don an oxygen mask. Lana, appalled, turned away. Arcane impatiently blew air between his lips and, once Rochelle had snapped off the disposal unit, said impatiently, "One more afternoon like this, Rochelle, and it's back to Betty Ford for you."

In confusion, Rochelle said, "Doctor, please . . . there's no need for the clinic."

"Not the clinic," said Lana. "He'll turn you *into* Betty Ford."

Rochelle stared from Lana to Arcane uncomfortably, then tried to force a laugh. The best he could manage was an uncertain cackle. "That's . . . that's very funny, sir." Privately he didn't think so. Even more privately he wondered whether Arcane was really joking or not.

"Kee-rist! What died in here?"

Arcane glanced around to see that Johnny Gunn, his security head, had entered, wrinkling his nose in exaggerated disgust.

Even by Arcane's standards, Johnny Gunn (which was probably not his real name) was distasteful. Over his jumpsuit he wore a black leather jacket, and the suit itself was unzipped down to the navel, displaying what he undoubtedly fancied to be a manly expanse of chest hair. He kept one thumb perpetually tucked in his belt, and his other hand was always dangling agitatedly near his holster, as if he couldn't wait for the slightest excuse to pull his gun. His unwashed black hair hung down to the back of his neck. His face was round and harsh, his black Vandyke beard ill kempt and untrimmed. From one ear dangled an axe-shaped earring.

"A cockroach died, Mr. Gunn," said Arcane calmly.

"Well, next time just use a roach motel, and it won't stink up the joint." He chucked a thumb in the direction of the elevator with which Arcane had descended to the laboratory. "Better get up there. Jerk-off sheriff wants to ask you what you know about what's been going on in the swamp."

"I?" Arcane professed surprise. "I am but a

humble scientist, trying to go about my business. That should be simple enough to understand."

"Yeah, well, you better explain it to him. 'Fore he starts poking around and I have to shoot him, and then you get to explain to the law that you've turned the sheriff into God knows what."

"Your point is well taken, Mr. Gunn." Without a further word he left the lab.

It was only once Arcane had departed that Rochelle realized he hadn't let out a breath in the last five minutes. Even Lana was shaking her head.

"He's getting more and more desperate," said Lana. "He needs the girl—Abigail."

"Right, right . . . the stepdaughter." Gunn pulled out a cigarette, but Lana quickly reached out to snatch it from him. Just as quickly Gunn intercepted her by the wrist, holding her hand away from it.

"No smoking down here," she said tersely. "There's oxygen in the next room. And let go of my hand."

They glared at each other for a moment and, still not releasing her, Gunn studied her carefully and said, "I hear tell you were willing to lay it on the line to get the girl down here. Gave it your all to convince her shrink."

"Where did you hear those lies?" she spat out.

Gunn nodded in Rochelle's direction. Zurrell turned slowly and gave Rochelle a venomous stare. Rochelle shrugged helplessly. "It kind of slipped out," he said apologetically.

"True, then?" asked Gunn, smirking.

Lana forcibly yanked her wrist out of Gunn's grasp, although he just as much let it go, and she rubbed it gingerly as she said, with an intense sincerity, "I would do anything for Dr. Arcane."

"Yeah, I'm getting that feeling." Gunn allowed the unlit cigarette to dangle from his chapped mouth. "Look, why go to all that trouble? Arcane wants the girl; me and a couple of guys could've gone to wherever she is and brought her down here, whether she wanted to go or not."

Slowly, even with a sort of bemused sorrow, Lana said, "Dr. Arcane has a blind spot when it comes to Abigail. He loved her mother and, by extension, the daughter. He does not want to take any hostile, forcible action against her. The doctor is a firm believer in the movings of fate. He would not force Abigail to come here and be a part of his . . . work. However, if the girl were to come here on her own, then he would accept that as the hand of destiny."

"I see. So he doesn't see any harm in 'guiding' destiny's hand just a little."

"That is correct."

Gunn shook his head. "And all this because he'd never harm his stepdaughter."

"Well . . ."—Lana smiled coldly—" 'never' is a long time."

"And that's the long and short of it, Doc."

They were in Arcane's study, ornately decorated in walnut with gold trim. Hung along the walls were mounted, stuffed heads of animals. Sheriff Beaumont glanced up at an elephant's head and couldn't shake the disturbing feeling that the glass eyes were staring back at him.

Beaumont forced his attention to Arcane, who was sitting behind his desk like a patient spider, eyes glistening alertly. "The man came hightailin' it out of the swamp and went straight for the Wein Motel—y'know, the creepy place with the spooky Brit running it?"

"I never go there, Sheriff," said Arcane.

"Yeah, well, anyways, this feller—Dugan's his name—spins this wild yarn about comin' out here nearby your property and runnin' across this giant leech thing. Claims it got two of his pals . . . sucked 'em dry right there on the spot."

"On the spot, you say?" Arcane asked, looking thoughtful, as if the concept of a leech creature were new to him.

Beaumont had a small pad he was consulting his notes from, and he glanced at it for verification. "Well, *he* says it, anyway. Also claims he was himself pulled," and he gave the words what he fancied to be a dramatic reading, "from the jaws of death by something that sounds to me like the man from Mars."

Arcane raised an eyebrow. "A man from Mars?"

"It's a planet, y'know," said Beaumont helpfully.

"You don't say."

A security woman, Tasha Pointsetta ("Points"

for short), clad in a tight, form-fitting black uniform, her brunette hair falling about her shoulders, served the sheriff a Dr Pepper. Beaumont looked her up and down and clearly liked what he saw both ways. "Thanks, honey. Got yourself a reg-u-lar Playboy mansion 'round here, don't'cha, Doc."

"Things are not always what they appear, Sheriff," said Arcane, ignoring the bristling Tasha. "For example, the most striking woman on my staff—no offense, Miss Pointsetta—would be Dr. Lana Zurrell. And she is a highly trained scientist, one of the world's leading specialists in the construction of human genes."

Beaumont laughed coarsely. "If she's anything like this one . . ."—he chucked a thumb at Points—"she can get into my jeans anytime."

As Beaumont snickered, Points reached toward the outstretched thumb, clearly ready to break it. Arcane, however, raised a silent, dissuading finger, waggling it slightly to indicate his disapproval. Annoyed, Points turned and left.

Arcane forced a polite smile. "You're a regular stand-up comedian, Sheriff. Tell me . . . was there any evidence of swamp mud found on this man?"

"He was covered with it," said Beaumont, forcing himself back to the subject that had brought him there.

"I'll tell you what happened. These men probably lost their way, fell into the bog, and all died—except for Dugan."

"But, dang it, how does that explain this guy's wild story?"

Arcane stood slowly and began to circle his desk as if trying to put together a reasonable explanation for unreasonable events. "He was submerged. The supply of oxygen to his brain was cut off and . . ." He paused and then snapped his fingers. ". . . And he hallucinated about giant leeches attacking him. Fortunately, at the last moment, he discovered a root and pulled himself to the surface. He saw the moss-covered tree, continued to hallucinate, and imagined the man from Mars. He then ran screaming into town like a madman."

Arcane stopped his pacing and stood there, hands spread, as if he'd just completed a gymnastic feat. Beaumont nodded thoughtfully and then flipped his notebook closed. "That sure makes sense . . . more sense than the crazy story. I suppose I should thank you. You may have saved me a couple thousand hours worth of investigation." He paused and then his eyes narrowed, curious to see Arcane's reaction as he added, "Of course I've still got to perform a search of the property, you understand."

From seemingly nowhere, Gunn materialized, the unlit cigarette still dangling from his mouth.

Look around all you wish, fool, thought Arcane; you'll never find any of the secret elevators down to the lab where the serious experiments are being done. Out loud he said, "Certainly," and waved in Gunn's direction. "Mr. Gunn here will show you around."

Beaumont grinned lopsidedly. "I'd much prefer one of the ladies."

"Of course," said Arcane. He gestured, and Gunn stepped aside.

Beaumont turned, the grin still on his face, and then it froze there as he looked up, and up.

The woman towered over him, massive and powerful, her lip in a perpetual sneer. She clapped a hand on his shoulder, and he lost all feeling in it.

"Uh uh uh," said Arcane scoldingly, "take good care of him."

The female guard nodded once and walked off, Beaumont in tow. The moment Beaumont was out of earshot Arcane turned quickly toward Gunn and said, "Holland is alive in the swamp."

At first, so unexpected was the statement, Gunn thought he was talking about the country of Holland. Then he understood. "It's not possible," said Gunn calmly, lighting up the cigarette. "My men combed very inch of that swamp."

"Well, comb it again. And you're not looking for a human being. You're looking for a plant."

Gunn snickered at that. "Maybe he married an avocado."

"Yes, and moved to California," said Arcane impatiently. "Just find Holland."

Suddenly the walkie-talkie hanging from Gunn's belt beeped. He unclipped it and put it to his ear. As he did, a bookcase in the study suddenly slid aside as Drs. Zurrell and Rochelle stepped out of the hidden elevator.

Even as the bookcase slid closed, Arcane turned on them with barely contained fury. "That was utterly brainless. What if the sheriff were still sitting here?"

"Sorry," said Rochelle.

"Sorry. You can keep your sorries. What I need is—"

"Hey, Doc . . . Holland will have to wait," said Gunn quickly. "There's a cab at the gate with a woman in it. She claims to be your stepdaughter."

Arcane's eyes widened. "Good God! Abigail!"

Arcane crossed quickly to the large bay window and looked out.

For a moment he thought it was Abby's mother stepping out of the cab. His breath caught. Then slowly he composed himself, turned, and said, "Dr. Rochelle . . . I've just been hit by an idea. Should Abigail have the same genetic code as her mother, I think we could be in business. Don't you agree?"

Rochelle looked at Lana in confusion. Why was Arcane talking as if Abigail's presence were a surprise, when in fact Arcane had orchestrated the entire plan that had brought her down?

Because, he realized, that was the way Arcane was. Possessor of secret knowledge, esoteric. He certainly endeavored to live up to his name.

All right. He, Rochelle, could play that game, too, "Yes, indeed," he said.

"Have a blood sample taken from her."

"How do we do that?" asked Rochelle.

Arcane took a step toward him, his eyes narrowing almost to invisibility. "You find a way."

"Yes, sir," said Rochelle in a small voice.

Then Arcane turned and draped a friendly arm around Lana. "Lana, I want you to make sure Abigail is taken care of beautifully. She must be considered as our prized possession."

And Lana, for no reason she could immediately determine, felt a wave of jealousy toward Abby. She couldn't even form the words. All she could manage was a curt nod.

The cabbie refused to go through the gate. And the guard wouldn't leave his post to help her. So it was that Abigail Arcane hauled her bag from the cab and, drenched with sweat, watched the cab speed away out of sight into the marsh.

She stepped through the large iron gate, and it slammed shut behind her.

For a moment . . . there was something.

A gentle feeling . . . as a butterfly on a leaf . . . a mind brushing against mine . . . someone . . . or something . . . that is at harmony . . . with nature.

Only a moment . . . and then it vanished . . . as if it fell . . . into a great and dark pit.

I have lost it . . . and suddenly . . . I no longer feel whole.

7

Abby toted the bag all the way to the steps leading up to the elaborate porch before the last of her strength gave out. She dropped the bag and an instant later dropped down next to it, certain she was about to collapse altogether from heat prostration.

"Abigail!"

She looked up, knowing the voice before she saw the owner.

He looked more like a reptile than he ever had as he trotted down the steps toward her. What in the name of God had her mother ever seen in the guy?

Just behind Arcane trotted another man, a man with a short beard who looked like a thug. He smiled at her the way a fox smiled at a rabbit.

Arcane embraced her, and she felt herself shrinking inwardly. "What a wonderful surprise," he whispered in her ear. "You've grown. You look marvelous."

And you look like death warmed over. "Well . . . how ya doing?" she asked, stepping back from him and forcing a smile. She glanced over the exterior of the house, her eyes settling once more on Gunn before taking in the other half-dozen guards she suddenly realized were lurking in the woodwork. "Nice place."

If he noted the sarcasm, he didn't show it. "Yes, a remarkable example of antebellum architecture, don't you think?"

Now Abby saw two other people, both in lab coats, step out onto the porch. A man and a woman. The woman looked like the classic ice bitch. The man reminded her of the kids she'd known in grade school who liked to pick the wings and legs off flies.

"Please, let's go inside. Mr. Gunn . . ."—he addressed the thug—"please bring my daughter's . . . my stepdaughter's," he amended, anticipating her correction, "bags."

Gunn nodded curtly and took the steps down two at a time. He grinned at Abigail, and she got the distinct impression that whatever he was thinking when he looked at her, it didn't involve her being clothed.

Now Arcane was gesturing toward the two lab-coated people. "Let me introduce you to some of my collaborators."

As Abby approached them she saw more clearly the insignia on their coats. It seemed to be a stylized *A*, and perched atop it was an eagle or some bird of prey, its wings outstretched. Abby could easily imagine herself caught in the bird's talons.

Dammit, you're trying to make peace with the man. Stop seeing threats everywhere you look.

"This is Lana Zurrell," he was saying. "*Dr.* Zurrell. She's my right hand. Doctor, this is my stepdaughter, Abigail."

Abby forced herself to put out a hand. Lana let it simply dangle there as she said icily, "Hello."

Battle lines are clearly drawn, thought Abby.

"And this is Dr. Rochelle."

Rochelle immediately took the proffered hand, and his whole body seemed to be trembling with excitement. "An extreme pleasure," he said.

"Brilliant man," Arcane said. "Does wonders with genetics."

"Your stepfather and I hope to be able to reverse the aging process!" burbled Rochelle.

"Yes . . . reverse completely," said Arcane, and he sounded extremely annoyed. Nevertheless he quickly brought back his air of pleasantry as he said, "Now, Abigail, this is your home. I want you to be comfortable, cozy, and happy. Get yourself settled, and we'll have dinner together tonight."

"Of course."

He squeezed her hand affectionately. "Lana will show you to your room."

Lana looked singularly unenthused about the assignment, but she merely nodded her head slightly and gestured for Abby to follow her. Abby took one last glance around as she entered the house and saw Arcane standing in a relaxed pose next to Rochelle.

Weird place, she thought.

The moment she was gone, Arcane turned and struck Rochelle.

The scientist fell to the ground, clutching at his split lip. He tried to stammer out a question.

"We hope to be able to reverse the aging process?!" Arcane stood over him, trembling with fury. "What were you thinking? *Were* you thinking?"

"Lana—"

"Lana what?"

Rochelle spat out blood. His words already sounded thick and uncomfortable. "She said if Abby asked, that's what I should say. That it was close enough to the truth so I could make it sound convincing. I'm not good at lying. You know that."

"But she didn't ask, did she?"

"Well . . . no . . ."

"You said it so quickly, unasked, that it looks like we're covering up something here."

"Well, we are—unnnhh!" Arcane had just kicked him in the side. He rolled over, nursing his ribs.

"Not . . . one . . . word," he said, each word hanging sizzling in the air. "Just keep your damned mouth shut, or so help me I'll take surgical staples and attend to your mouth myself. Understood?"

Rochelle managed a weak nod as Arcane turned from him in disgust and strode into the mansion.

Abby walked into the room and turned slowly, staring in disbelief. With its elaborate canopy bed and ornate, carved furniture, it looked like a room Scarlett O'Hara would have been comfortable in.

Gunn preceded her, carrying the bag, and Lana followed her. To make sure I don't make a break for it? she wondered.

Gunn threw the bag on the bed, turned, tossed off a mock salute, and strode from the room. Lana trailed a finger along one of the dresser tops, checking for dust she knew would not be there. "This should be satisfactory."

"It's very pretty," said Abby, and then she turned and directed her next remark at Lana, "like everything my stepfather owns."

Now, why did I say that? she wondered. That's really catty. I'm not like that. It's like this place brings out the worst in me.

Lana, utterly nonplussed, replied, "Your stepfather has excellent taste."

Abby sat on the edge of the bed, trying to appraise Lana. "He's kind of strange, isn't he?"

"Dr. Arcane is a great man, a genius. Sometimes you have to indulge greatness."

Good God! That's almost word for word what my mother used to say about him! What is he, a hypnotist?

Abby's eyes narrowed. Let's see if I can get a

rise out of her. Maybe break through whatever spell he's cast.

"Is that your job here?" she asked coyly. "To indulge him?"

"My job," Lana said, bristling, "is to assist your stepfather in any way I can. He is an exacting man, as I'm sure you'll see, and one who demands obedience from those around him."

"Why is it I think you enjoy that?" Abby said, toying with a strand of her hair.

"We have a unique relationship."

"I'll just bet you do."

Lana took a step forward, apparently seething inside. "You are a rude girl who barges in unannounced on a very busy man and disrupts his important work."

Direct hit. "Important work? So I've heard."

"I gave up my post at the world's foremost genetics research center to work with your father on a great humanitarian project."

Abby gaped at her incredulously. "Are we talking about the same man?" Now she rose from the bed and walked toward Lana. Her voice took on a hard, bitter edge. "You can call my stepfather a lot of things, but I doubt 'humanitarian' is one of them."

"You don't know him as I do."

They were now almost nose-to-nose, and in a low, angry tone, Abby said, "I know he screwed up my childhood."

They stared at each other for a long moment, neither backing down. Then, abruptly, Lana Zurrell dropped her gaze and said, "Will you be staying long?"

"What's it to you?"

"I think," and this time she sounded almost withdrawn, "if you have any more questions, you better ask Dr. Arcane."

She turned and strode quickly out the door.

Abby stood there, shaking her head. She had definitely gotten some sort of reaction out of Zurrell. The problem was, she wasn't exactly sure what the reaction was.

She went back to the bed, picked up the bag, and started to unpack it. As she did she became aware something was missing . . . something gnawing at the back of her mind, something that by its very absence was making her edgy and uncertain.

Then she realized what it was: plant life. There were no plants, not only in the room, but throughout all of the house she had thus far seen. Usually large houses like this had potted plants, ferns, something.

She'd never been to the mansion before. Arcane had always come to visit her and her mother in California. Although Abby's mother had been captivated by him, Abby had always felt overwhelming revulsion. When, after several years, Abby's mother had married Arcane and moved down to the Louisiana compound, Abby had steadfastly refused to visit. It had been her greatest frustration in life that she had never managed to convince her mother of the pure evil in the man.

Yet now here she was, in the house of her enemy. . . .

And where were the goddamn plants? It wasn't just in the house, she realized. The entire exterior grounds—and they were not inconsiderable—had been paved off. Not so much as a blade of grass grew anywhere. The only trees that existed were beyond the perimeter.

She looked out her window at the darkening sky. The trees formed a ghostly skyline in the distance, and beyond that, she saw a mountain peak, towering tall and majestic. Its craggy surface had more personality to it than any of the walking zombies in the mansion.

She sighed deeply and finished her unpacking. When, a short time later, a security guard brought dinner up to her room, offering Arcane's excuses that he was feeling under the weather, she was actually grateful.

She pulled out a copy of *A Tree Grows in Brooklyn* and sat down to read. She couldn't help but notice there were no greens on her plate.

Lightning danced an electric pirouette of death across the night sky.

At night the mansion looked far more like a prison compound than a genteel Southern household. Security guards slowly patrolled the grounds, on the watch for everything and anything.

From his bedroom window, clad in a silk dressing gown, Arcane stared out at the swamp, like a monarch surveying his domain.

Except . . .

He knew whose domain it was.

Somewhere out there, Holland was lurking, planning and plotting.

It had been several years since their previous encounter. Several years since he, Arcane, had come staggering from the swamp. His body had been misshapen, transformed into that of a beast from the bowels of hell. He had been mortally wounded, his life pouring out of a chest wound inflicted on him by Holland.

By the "man from Mars." By the Swamp Thing.

He had staggered in through the secret entrance known only to two people—himself and Dr. Rochelle. And sure enough, Rochelle had been waiting as a torn and bleeding Arcane, his body blue and encrusted with scales, his hair long and wild, his face completely unrecognizable, made it back to the lab.

He would have died right there, gotten all the way back to the lab only to expire on the sterile floor, except for the thing he'd been clutching like a lifeline in his hand.

A clump of moss, tangled weed . . . a piece of the Swamp Thing, torn unknowingly from the bog creature's side during their battle.

This clump of moss was imbued with the bio-restorative formula that had salvaged the burning near-corpse of Alec Holland those years ago and preserved his life. It was a shambling, moss-encrusted mockery of life, but life nevertheless.

Hooking up Arcane to life-support systems, Rochelle had worked feverishly, using previously drawn tissue samplings from Arcane, analyzing and breaking down his genetic structure, and combining it with all the formula he had managed to extract from the samplings of the Swamp Thing.

The resultant mixture had been injected into the dying body of Anton Arcane.

And it had worked.

Sort of.

Arcane remembered lying there on the table, naked and dazed and being told by Rochelle that he, Arcane, had been brought back from the brink of death by a scientific miracle.

But it was not, he feared, permanent.

Arcane had been changed, mutated. Although he bore the semblance of human form, his entire structure was now a genetic time bomb. As years wore on it would inevitably start to break down, regress, either back into his animal form or worse, if such a phenomenon could be imagined.

Endeavors to synthesize more of the biorestorative formula from the sampling of Swamp Thing proved ineffectual. Separated from the host body, the samples had dried out, become useless.

Arcane had begun searching for the Swamp Thing once again, for if he could capture the creature, he could create a lifetime's worth of biorestorative elixir from the former Alec Holland. But the Swamp Thing was not to be found. It was as if, having supposedly settled accounts with Arcane, the creature had simply vanished. Perhaps, Arcane realized, the Swamp Thing had lost the will to live upon realizing humanity was to be forever denied him. Perhaps he had simply rotted away.

Or perhaps he was out there, lurking, waiting. Arcane began to reflect upon the creature's possibilities, upon the power that might be his to command. Such reflection made Arcane exceedingly nervous. And so he had stripped all the grounds of any greenery, afraid of what the plant life might do to him. And when months of searching proved fruitless, Arcane decided the Fates were trying to tell him something.

And so Arcane had turned his attention to genetic research to stave off the deterioration always lurking in the back of his mind, like a cancer rotting him away. . . .

"Something wrong?"

He turned slowly in response to the low female voice behind him.

Lana stepped out of the shadows, dressed in a negligee that left nothing to the imagination, or to chance.

"I don't see anything wrong," said Arcane in a low voice.

She seemed to glide toward him. "I'm delighted."

There was a low rumble of thunder that appeared to accompany her sultry movement.

"In fact, I like what I see very much," said Arcane. And what I don't see . . . even more." He paused. "Don't move."

She stayed where she was as he circled around her. From behind her he said, "Yes, this angle is very good, too."

He reached out toward her . . .

. . . and stopped.

He stared frozenly at his hand. He held up the other one. Both were cracked and dry.

Lana sensed the change in mood and turned. For a moment she regained her clinical composure. "You're not showing signs yet, are you?"

He brushed off the concern he himself felt. "Maybe just a difference in texture."

She took one of his hands in either of hers, studying them with concern. Then, slowly, she took them and placed them against her breasts.

"We'll find some way to reverse the aging," she whispered. "I'll never let anything happen to you."

"Lana." His voice choked with passion. "Lana . . ."

"Just stay vital, my darling." She raised his hands up, kissing them with each word. "I . . . need . . . you . . . vital."

She pulled his robe open even as he drew her toward the bed. The robe, and her nightgown, fell away.

Outside the lightning flashed brighter; the thunder cracked louder.

• • •

Abby was running.

In the darkness, in the blackness of the eerie house that looked familiar, yet different, she was running for her life . . . and for someone else's life.

A dizzying stairway stretched down before her, trailing off down to infinity. She hesitated, but whatever was pursuing her from behind was drawing closer, ever closer, and she couldn't hesitate. She dashed down the stairway, trying to feel her way as best she could.

She looked down and suddenly realized she was naked. Before she could figure it out, her feet went out from under her and she fell headlong down the stairs. She threw her arms out, trying to catch hold of something, but there was nothing to halt her fall, and she tumbled, end over end, stairs smashing into her head, bruising her body, before she hit the bottom. She lay there shivering on the cold marble, scrambling about, muttering, "Green. Please . . . something green . . ."

A voice called to her from above, at the top of the stairs. She turned and froze in shock.

"Mother . . . ?" she whispered.

"Yes, baby." She stood there, arms open. "I'm waiting for you. Please help me."

And Abby turned, not questioning her nudity, not questioning what her mother was doing at the top of the stairs, and she started to run up the stairway she'd just taken a harrowing plunge down. She picked up speed, taking them two at a time, yet she didn't seem to be getting any closer.

At the top of the stairs her mother was starting to change color. Her skin was becoming frozen blue, icicles forming on her hair and eyebrows, frost crusting her lips, her eyes staring open and dead, and still she whispered, "Abby . . . help me."

With a final frantic leap Abby vaulted to the top of the stairs and threw her arms around her mother. There was a crackle, an unholy splintering, as her mother's body cracked and crumbled into a thousand shards of ice.

Abby screamed, but there was no sound.

She looked down the hallway. To the left was a railing that separated the landing from a drop into nothingness. On the right was a long blank wall with a single open door. At her feet her mother's frozen head lay intact, and she grabbed up the head and dashed down the hallway, shouting, "Please help her! Help my mother!"

She entered the room, which was illuminated by lightning. The only thing in it was a bed, and in the bed were Arcane and Lana, bodies intertwined. They didn't even notice her as she screamed, thrusting her mother's head in front of her, water dripping from it. "You were married to her! You said you loved her! You have to help her!"

Arcane's rhythmic movements atop Lana began to slow, and he turned his reptilian gaze on Abby.

Outside the window lightning flashed, and a hideous death's head visage appeared over Arcane's face. A burning skull flashed eyes of lambent green, and the skinless mouth laughed at her.

With a scream Abby dropped her mother's head, and it crashed to the floor, breaking beyond repair. Abby backed out of the room, feet crunching on the ice that had been her mother, not taking her eyes from Arcane's hideous face.

Her back hit the railing, and she remembered too late the drop awaiting her. She tried to find support, but it was too late and she flipped over the railing and fell, a long, high shriek the only thing that followed her as she plummeted, plummeted . . .

Something caught her.

Instinctively she reached out, clutching at whatever it was that had saved her. She came away with fistfuls of leaves, and dirt under her fingernails. And now her nostrils were filled with the sweet smell of lime, and her soul was filled with the eternal peace of the earth.

She was being cradled in two massive arms, arms covered with vines and moss, and she looked up into a face that was not a face. The mouth was obscured by darkness—she could barely discern the top of the head. The only features she could make out were the eyes, small and red, floating in a pool of black.

He spoke to her then, every word an effort, as

if he were trying to remember how one moved one's mouth.

"You called . . . for the green . . . and I came to you."

She reached, feeling the blissful peace of his massive chest. "How did you know where to find me?" she whispered.

"I . . . did not . . . know. I felt . . . the essence of you . . . but I did not know . . . do not know . . . the where of you. . . ."

"I'm . . . I'm here," she said. "Wherever 'here' is."

She stepped down from his arms, slowly, and they were surrounded by blackness, but with him there was solidity, there was no fear.

"You . . . are not afraid . . . of me?"

Slowly she shook her head as she pressed her naked body against his. "I love you," she whispered. "How couldn't I love you? I've been looking for you all my life."

She felt vines beginning to surround her . . . and suddenly he stopped, and she felt him growing distant from her. "What's wrong?" she said urgently.

"There is evil . . . abroad in the swamp . . . this night," he said, looking off toward some point beyond where she could see. "I must attend . . . to it."

"Come back!" She started to tremble. "Don't leave me! I need you!"

"Come to me," he said. "In the swamp . . . but not this night. Not until the evil . . . is gone."

"When, then?!"

His body began to crumble in her arms, falling away, rotting. And from all around her a voice said, "Soon."

And a name came to her, a name she didn't know.

She cried out, *"Alec!"*

Arcane paused above Lana, frowning. He could have sworn he'd just heard Abigail shout out from her room, scream out Holland's name. He shrugged and went back to feigning passion.

Abigail sat up, the name still frozen on her lips.

She looked around frantically, confused, disoriented as one always is when one wakes up in a strange place.

Within moments she realized she was still in the bedroom Arcane had assigned her. It was dark out, the night sky alive with lightning and thunder.

She had thrashed about so much, she had twisted herself completely around in her sheets. Slowly she untangled herself, stepped out of bed, and adjusted the simple white shift she was wearing. Normally she slept naked, but somehow coming here she had wanted the questionable protection a nightgown afforded her.

She went to the window and looked out. The night sky had cracked open, and rain was pouring down in waves. Far in the distance that mountain peak seemed to reign over all the land around it. She imagined that there, atop the mountain, sat perched the great god of the swamps . . . looking down, rendering judgment.

Flashes of her dream returned to her. Her mother, Arcane, the faintest of memories, already mercifully vanishing.

And something else. Something massive, something with the sweet smell of vegetation, the sharp taste of lime, and the strength of the earth in massive limbs.

And the name she had screamed in her dream, now, just speaking it softly, brought peace to her, a sense that she was not alone.

"Alec," she whispered.

I felt her. . . .

Earth mother . . . who is she . . . ?

I sense her purity . . . and beauty of spirit . . . and her oneness . . . with nature.

Unlike the other humans . . . of flesh and meat . . . she remembers the times when humankind . . . depended on the green . . . for survival. A time before pollutants . . . and defoliation.

The beauty of humankind . . . lives within her . . . and she does not know. All she knows . . . is that she is unhappy . . . in the human world . . . just as I find . . . growing discontent . . . living only in the world . . . of the green.

Perhaps we can . . . provide each other . . . a mutual bridging of . . . our worlds . . . for without her . . . I am not whole.

But first . . . I must attend . . . to the unnatural one.

8

A dozen letters were already burnt out in the sign, and several more were flickering dangerously near to extinction. In its heyday the sign had read in full UNCLE SHED'S RIVER GARDEN ESTATES. WHERE THE BYWAY MEETS THE BAYOU. NO REASONABLE RATE REFUSED. DAILY-WEEKLY-MONTHLY.

Of course, even when the sign had been at its best, it couldn't begin to hide the true nature of the "estates": namely that it was no more than a series of run-down, off-road bungalows barely one notch up from a crummy trailer park (and indeed, several notches below a really nice trailer park).

All the bungalows looked basically alike, yet this rainy night a long figure scooted through the Estates, making his way through the barely lit blackness with practiced quickness.

He was aware of the late hour, aware if his parents found out he had sneaked out in the middle of the night, they'd rip the hide off his butt, aware (painfully) that his sneakers had completely filled up with water.

He was not aware of the hideous malevolence that watched him from the edge of the grounds.

He got to the bungalow he sought and pounded on the door. He'd been trying for subterfuge, not wanting to rouse anyone in the pathetic group of bungalows. But with his goal so near he was becoming very impatient. And very soggy.

"Hey, Omie, it's me! Let me in! It's pourin' out here," he added somewhat unnecessarily.

There was some scuffling from within, and the door opened slightly, held by a chain lock. From inside, Omar Brown, who lived in the bungalow when he wasn't out dodging the sheriff's car, stared out at his waterlogged friend.

And hesitated, realizing if you can't torture a waterlogged friend, who can you torture? Hey! Water torture!

"Well, ain't'cha gonna let me in?" said Darryl, for such was the name of the young man who was outside.

"Looks kinda wet out there," observed Omar.

"You're damn straight it is! Now open the stupid door and let me in."

And in a dazzling example of twelve-year-old humor, Omar asked, "What's the password?"

"Password!" squealed Darryl. "Whaddaya mean, password? We never had a password!"

"Got one now" was the serene reply.

Darryl squeezed his fingers into a small fist. "You wanna password. I'll give you a password."

"Oh, I'm soooo scared," said Omar in his best Pee-Wee Herman voice. He grinned inwardly and then watched as Darryl backed up a few feet, now desperate enough to transform his stout body into a human battering ram.

"All right, you!" said Darryl with more confidence than he felt. "Here . . . I . . . come!"

Omar's timing was perfect, waiting until Darryl was at full-committal speed before swinging wide the door and announcing, "Hey, that's the password!"

Darryl shot full-speed into the bungalow, tripping as he tried to stop his charge and succeeding only in tumbling over a coffee table.

That his friend might have split his head open never occurred to Omar. He was too busy chuckling.

Darryl pulled himself upright with annoyance and what little dignity he could muster. "You jerk!" was the best insult he could come up with.

"You're a double jerk."

"No, you are." With the opening salutations out of the way, Darryl looked around suspiciously. "Your folks gone?"

"Course," said Omar confidently. "Weekend trip. Won't be back for ages. You can stay over if you want."

"Damned straight, 'cause I'm not going back out there, no way," said Darryl, sliding off his rain slicker. He tried his best to restore some order to his orange hair. "Then you got 'em?"

"Do I got 'em?" replied Omar, feigning insult.

"Well, let's see 'em."

"Be cool, bro', be cool," said Omar in his best *Miami Vice* tone. "Don't get your bowels in an uproar." His voice taking on the tone of a confident bartender, he said, "What are ya drinkin'?"

Moments later, the rain rattling noisily on the tin roof overhead, the boys were guzzling down Pepsi as if it had been outlawed and noisily blasting music videos on the fuzzy black-and-white TV.

Omar came out of the forbidden territory, his father's room, under the bed, inside his dad's old footlocker, from which he had withdrawn a dazzling array of reading material. He dumped the pile unceremoniously in front of Darryl.

"There ya have it. The year in pictures," he crowed. "Dig in."

It was a truly impressive assortment. Every issue in the past twelve months of every smutty, sleazy girlie magazine obtainable in Lacroix, Louisiana, was scattered on the floor. For once obeying his friend to the letter, Darryl promptly dropped to his knees and dug in.

He went through the foldouts with the alacrity of a speed-reader. The truth was, while the *Playboy* magazines, for example, were easy on the eyes, some of the others had women posed in positions that were not only unattractive, but downright uncomfortable to look at. He would be damned, however, if he would let his friend know any of the pictures were distasteful. No way was he gonna let Omar think he was a wuss.

So, summoning up what he imagined passed as a macho voice, Darryl said, "Whoa, I can't believe it. Look at these babes."

"Check out the one in the June ish of *Young & Easy*. She's one of the old man's favorites."

Darryl did so, pulling out the suggested issue and surveying the centerfold. It was one of those ones that made his eyes ache. He didn't want to look at it, but Omar was watching him intently. "My God, she's . . ." Darryl floundered, his eyes darting, trying to find something on the page that was noninflammatory, and he lit on the handful of words lining the bottom. "She's . . . a Scorpio! And I'm an Aries! They get along great."

Omar grinned. "My man, I wouldn't steer you wrong."

Darryl smiled inwardly, certain he had maintained his cool in this extremely stressful situation. . . .

Then the pounding began on the door.

The boys looked at each other, a moment frozen in horror.

Inside of a split second, Omar's rigidly maintained cool crumbled as he leapt to his feet, trying to gather up all the magazines. "My parents! It's my parents! Put 'em away! Get 'em away!"

Magazines were falling out from between his arms. Darryl was running in place, yelling "Where? Where?" over the music videos.

"Anywhere! Anywhere! Just make 'em gone. Right away! Right away!"

Fearful of being caught holding one, Darryl madly kicked the ones on the floor out of sight beneath the couch. Omar ran into the bedroom and hurled them into the footlocker helter-skelter, slamming the box closed so quickly he caught the edges of a couple of the magazines.

The banging came from the door again as Omar shoved the footlocker under the bed. He envisioned his parents standing out in the rain, wondering what the hell was going on in there.

He dashed back out to find Darryl chugalugging the soda to get rid of the can (as if there was somethin' wrong with drinking soda!). "Be right there, Ma!" he shouted over the pounding. He went to Darryl quickly, clapped a hand on his shoulder, and, trying to pull together his own shaken confidence, said, "C'mon, take a chill pill, man—you look guilty as hell."

Darryl looked the way he felt as he tried to compose himself. "Just a sec," called Omar, who took one last quick glance around the room, then went to the door and undid the chain lock.

He swung wide the door.

The Leech was standing there, making sickly sucking noises with its mouth.

Omar tried to speak, tried to think of something to say, tried to find his voice. In the squeakiest of whispers he managed to get out, "Darryl . . . it's for you . . ."

With a low moan the Leech took a step forward, and that snapped Omar out of his paralysis. With a shriek, a shriek echoed by Darryl who was standing right behind him, he slammed the door shut and bolted the chain lock.

He turned, back against the door, feet braced, and shouted, "Help me keep it shut!"

A large, misshapen ebony fist smashed through just to the right of Omar's head. It tried to grab the boy, but Omar leapt away, his jump carrying him past Darryl, who was once again running in place, his mouth opening and closing with nothing coming out. Omar paused only long enough to grab Darryl by the front of his catsup-stained shirt, and they bolted out the back door.

Two seconds later the Leech had smashed the door off its hinges. It scanned the vacant room, and a howl of anger emerged through its inhuman mouth.

The boys darted outside, and Darryl skidded in the mud, falling flat. The rain poured down, matting down their hair in a matter of seconds as Omar yanked his friend to his feet and pointed off to the right. The bungalows on either side of Omar's family had been vacant, but there were inhabitants in the ones farther over.

They started toward those, somehow believing that merely being with adults would provide safety. Obviously they were being pursued by the bogeyman, after all, and the bogeyman only went after children.

They were less than halfway there when the Leech cut them off, stepping in their path from the shadows. Lightning crackled overhead, giving unearthly shading to the creature's already inhuman appearance.

The boys screamed, all pretensions of cool long since gone. They bolted in the other direction, toward where all the local cars were lined up, station wagons and four-by-fours and a large RV and all kinds of things, man-made metal monsters bearing silent witness to the activities of a different man-made monster.

The Leech was picking up speed behind the boys, fingers grabbing, and Omar suddenly felt it catch the trailing end of his shirt. He pulled free with a howl and crashed headlong into a tree that had not been there moments ago.

No. Not a tree . . .

Once again . . . this monstrosity stalks the swamps . . . as if it were entitled . . . to be part of . . . the natural order.

It is a belief . . . I must dissuade . . . now.

The Antibody promptly forgot the invaders it had been pursuing. Once again it was confronted by the mind and heart of the swamp. This time it knew there would be no negotiation, no moment of painful request for acceptance, followed by rejection. This time . . . there would be no mercy.

Omar looked from the Swamp Thing to the Leech and back again. "Hey, man, it's Monster Central around here"—saying that mostly because he thought it sounded good as famous last words.

But Darryl, who was not at all ready to utter his final syllables, said, "Cripes, I don't wanna die! I just reached puberty . . . I think."

And even as he spoke he yanked Omar by the collar and away from the two creatures he was sure had come to divide the two of them up, one kid per monster.

He heard an agonized grunt and paused only momentarily to glance over his shoulder and gape in astonishment.

The monsters weren't friends!

This was an interesting turn of events, he realized, as he and Omar ducked behind a bush for cover.

Swamp Thing stood there, patient as the great redwoods, as the Leech charged him, determined this time to overwhelm him by sheer brute force.

It was like a pebble trying to overwhelm a boulder. The Leech slammed into the Swamp Thing, certain the way to defeat him was to rip apart the vines, send the dirt flying, dig and dig, for somewhere within had to be veins it could suck dry, a living heart it could rip from a chest and drink the still-warm blood from.

Swamp Thing's only acknowledgment of the charge was a mild grunt as he reached down and lifted the Leech high over his head. He paused, prepared to toss the creature in one direction until he saw the boys in the line of fire, so he turned and hurled the Leech in the direction of the cars. The Leech smashed into an old DeSoto, crushing the hood and front fender.

It staggered to its feet, reeling from the impact as the Swamp Thing advanced on it. It reached down with its malformed hands to steady itself, its fingers wrapping around the front bumper.

Swamp Thing came closer, closer, with rain pouring down and his red eyes blazing with fury.

The Leech ripped the front bumper from the car and, with all its strength, smashed the bumper into the Swamp Thing's head.

The blow came with such force it decapitated the marsh monster, and his head went flying across the expanse of the grounds.

From the bushes Darryl and Omar let out a shriek in unison.

Swamp Thing's body thrashed around, confused and disoriented, and now it was the Leech that was closing on him, swinging the sharp-edged bumper with speed and fury. Unable to defend itself, the headless body fell quick victim to the Leech's merciless assault. Within seconds the ground was covered with dirt and weeds hacked out in huge chunks from the body. Determined to do a more thorough job than before, the Leech had also severed both arms, and now, with a massive windup, it swung through and sliced Swamp Thing's torso clean of the lower half of his body.

The legs staggered about helplessly for a moment, like a grotesque, stringless puppet, and then fell over lifeless.

The Leech stood there, chest heaving from its exertions, clutching the muck-covered bumper, and then it made the most inhuman sound of all. It laughed, the laugh of Satan when a new soul has been consigned to hell.

It turned then, glowering, its inhuman eyes resting on the two boys cowering behind the bush. It took one step toward them.

One step, and no more.

It paused in confusion and looked down.

Its foot had taken root. Or, more precisely, the roots had taken foot.

It yanked experimentally, unsure what was happening. It couldn't move its foot. Roots had grown from the ground, surrounding the Leech's foot in a deceptively gentle manner. The Leech yanked upward with more force, managing to raise its foot perhaps a few inches before the roots actually yanked the foot back down again.

And while it was concentrating on its left foot, its right one was also ensnared. Green vines stretched forth, working their way upward gracefully, and the Leech howled in confusion as it found its entire lower legs completely enveloped in plant life.

The growth swelled outward, beginning to take a form other than that of the Leech. The plant legs developed their own shape, musculature formed of the strongest wood fibers coming into existence. There were small, curious popping noises as leaves uncurled, slapping moistly against one another.

In one horrific moment the immobilized Leech realized what was happening. The monster of the green was reforming, growing a new body . . . and was doing so around the Leech.

With a scream of pure terror the Leech drew back its only weapon, the ripped-off car bumper, and started to pound furiously at its own body, trying to rid itself of the earthen invader. Clods of dirt were smashed away, but as quickly as they were, new ones took their place. And now the Leech was covered with the creeping grass all over its body, and ivy was stretching out and encompassing its arms as it began to lose mobility, and mud was filling its nostrils, and it couldn't breathe.

The world blacked over as the Swamp Thing's head formed over that of the Leech.

In a mad paroxysm of fear the Leech struggled with one last hysterical burst of energy. It had only seconds with which to act, for its air had been cut off. The Leech had literally been buried alive. It twisted; it fought even as it lost the ability to move its arms. Mud and sludge that had a life of its own worked its way into the Leech's mouth, started down for its lungs, slim tendrils beginning to probe. . . .

And trapped there, in the coolness of the dirt, someone else's life flashed before the Leech's eyes—a life that had been consumed by a woman with black hair and ivory skin, of heat and passion. . . .

The Leech ripped free.

One of its once-human appendages tore free from the mud, grasping for the air, and once finding the air, would not be denied. It wrenched its entire body, felt bones snapping, and somewhere inside it something was ripped out of place, but the Leech succeeded, tearing out of its vertical grave like the reborn vampire it had become.

It was covered with mud and muck, almost indistinguishable from the swamp creature it had been fighting. Incredibly it was still holding onto the bumper. It turned, staggering, sucking in lungfuls of air. From somewhere nearby it heard the dismayed cries of the two young boys, but they could wait. The Swamp Thing was its total concern now—the Swamp Thing it had killed once, and would kill over and over, as many times as it took.

The heavy rain washed away some of the dirt from its eyes, and it turned to see the Swamp Thing watching it from nearby, standing in front of the RV, the most notable feature of which was a large fading decal on the side of the Terminator with the inscription I'LL BE BACK in menacing letters.

The Leech pointed challengingly at the Swamp Thing and then shrieked as pain lanced through its shoulder. In its twists to break free it had dislocated its left arm.

The only time the Leech ever sounded human was when it was in agony, and it never sounded more human than it did now. Choking, it grabbed its left shoulder with its right hand, and somewhere in the back of its mind was some vestige of medical training as, howling and sobbing, it shoved the arm back into its socket.

It turned toward the Swamp Thing then, consumed with hatred and ache—ache for what it had gone through, and ache for what it had lost, which was beginning to return to it with a faint dimness.

The Leech charged, swinging the bumper back and forth like a great sword.

Swamp Thing watched it coming, and there was something in his eyes that could no longer exist in the Leech's eyes, or in the Leech's soul, as black and hell-blasted as that might be.

And just as the Leech was about to connect, Swamp Thing said with unutterable sadness, "I'm sorry."

He left his body, diving back into the green.

The Leech's makeshift weapon swung through the now-lifeless pile of weeds and fiber and struck what Swamp Thing had been standing directly in front of: propane tanks mounted on the sides of the RV. The Leech had a brief flash of the warning signs on the side of the tanks that read DANGER: CONTENTS UNDER PRESSURE, DO NOT PUNCTURE. They were warnings that had no meaning.

The tanks exploded.

Omar and Darryl, many yards away, were nevertheless knocked back by the force of the explosion. They shrieked in alarm and then from nowhere the bush they had been hiding behind grew larger, became an impenetrably thick shield of branches, blocking them from harm.

They heard a repeated series of explosions then, and realized the fire had spread to the other cars. Omar moaned. "Aw, shit, Mom's new station wagon," he said.

Shards of metal hurled through the air, smashing windows of bungalows, leaving trails like miniature comet tails through the night. Hundreds of them were hurled toward the boys, any one of which could have ended their young lives. Instead they buried themselves harmlessly in the bush that acted as the boys' protective screen. Before any of the flaming pieces could cause the growing matter to catch fire, the rain extinguished it.

The rain was helping to dampen the fire roaring from what had been a row of parked cars as well.

And then the boys heard a shriek.

They stood, miraculously being missed by the last bits of metal, in time to see a creature of pure fire emerge howling from the inferno.

Completely aflame, the Leech lurched out. It twisted and staggered like an out-of-control robot. Its face was starting to melt like a waxwork. Guttural, incomprehensible sounds emerged from what was left of its mouth. Its clothes had burned away completely to reveal a crispening, blackened, and distorted body.

It lunged toward the swamp, still screaming, instinctively pounding at itself to try and stop the flames, and then it hurled itself into the waters. A huge cloud of steam rose from where it had entered, and in less than a second it had sunk from sight.

And then the boys' view of the departed creature was blocked as the bush in front of them continued to grow. Insanely the bush twisted in and back on itself, taking on the vague shape of human features and appearance.

It stood and looked down at them with glowing red eyes.

Slowly Omar raised his hand and gave a thumbs-up. Darryl looked on with wide-eyed astonishment and then did the same thing.

The Swamp Thing looked from one to the other, stared at his own hand as if trying to recall that it, too, had once been human, and then clenched it and returned the gesture to the boys.

All around them now were shouts of confusion, people roused from their slumber by the explosions. Screams of "Fire!" and "Get the extinguishers!" abounded. The air was filled with heat, and the Swamp Thing felt the small leaves and branches of his body beginning to dry and crackle, a few trailing wisps of smoke rising from them.

As if afraid, he quickly tore the crisping leaves from himself and then strode off slowly into the shadows. He seemed to just melt into the trees as all around the boys now were adults in various states of undress, with hastily tossed-on robes or old sweat clothes, doing whatever they could to fight the fire. And there was that gorgeous babe who lived over in cabin six, wearing only a T-shirt and panties that were already becoming soaked through and you could see everything. . . .

Except Omar and Darryl were not paying the least bit of attention to the gorgeous babe. Even the magazines were forgotten. They were staring off into the shadows, and slowly Darryl summed it up.

"Awesome."

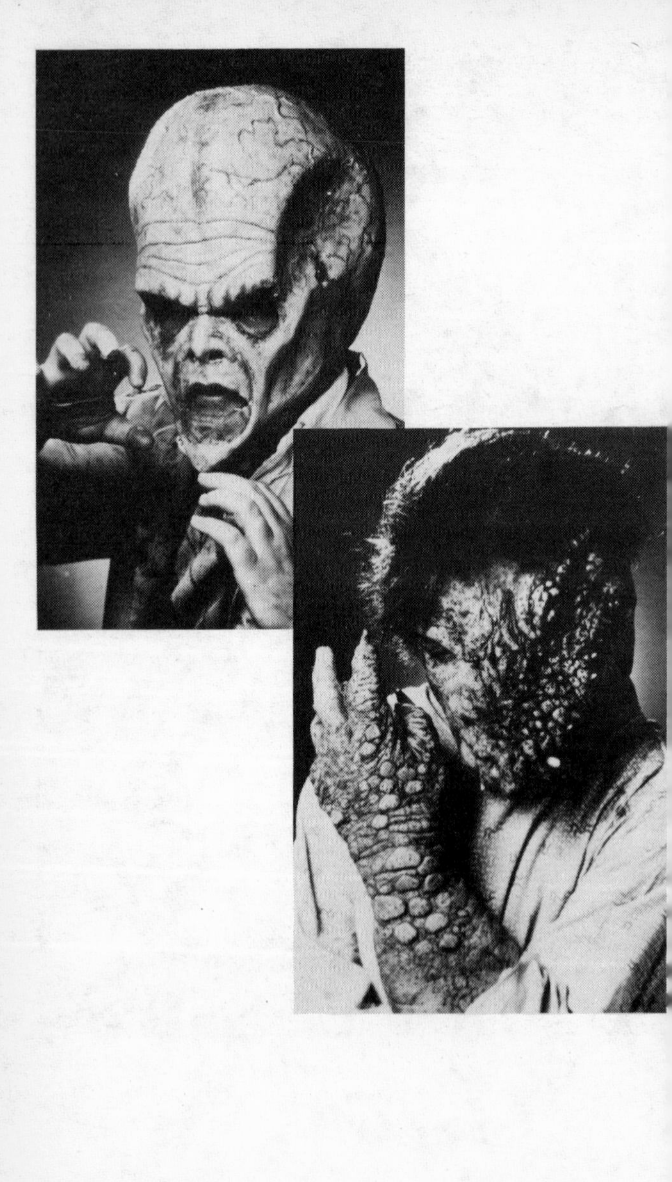

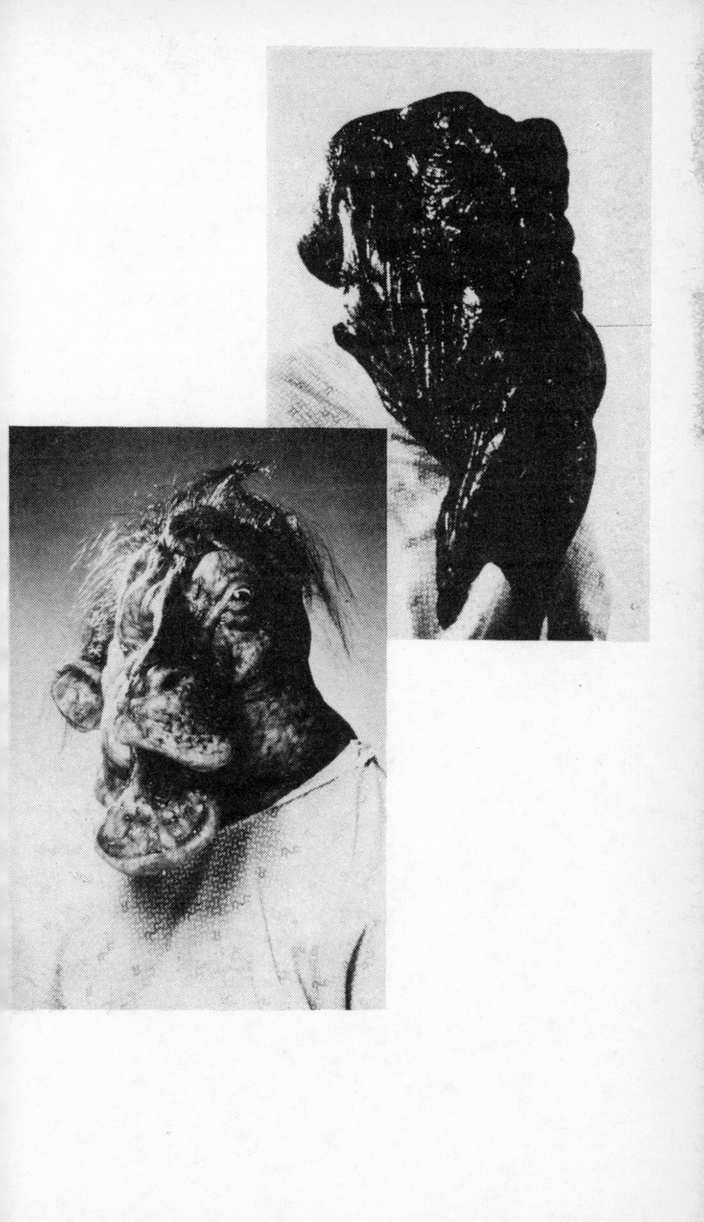

9

The sun was not completely able to cut through the gray clouds still hanging in the air. Somehow the gods never seemed to tire of threatening rain upon the beleaguered inhabitants of Suicide Swamp.

Arcane sat in bed, Lana sleeping deeply next to him. But the warmth of her body was forgotten as Arcane stared at the newspaper that had been left quietly, as always, at the foot of the bed.

The banner headline in that day's *Bayou Post* read LOCAL RESORT GOES BOOM. Below that, in smaller type, was LOCAL BOYS CLAIM THEY SAW NOTHING. There was a grainy photograph of two boys, a taller back boy who was clapping his hand over the mouth of a shorter, stockier white boy.

Moments later Arcane, dressing gown swirling around him like a dark cloud, strode through the hallway to find Gunn lounging against a decorative pillar, trying to make time with fellow security guard Tasha Points. As always, even though it was first thing in the morning, a cigarette was dangling from Gunn's mouth.

"Those things will turn on you someday," snapped Arcane.

Gunn tipped his beret mockingly. "Morning to you, too, Doc."

Arcane shoved the newspaper into the pit of Gunn's stomach. "Have you seen this?"

Gunn unfolded the paper and stared at it uncomprehendingly. He read: "IRATE FANS LYNCH STEINBRENNER. Well, hell, it's about time."

"Not the sports pages, you imbecile," snapped Arcane, switching the paper around.

This time Gunn scanned the appropriate article, but clearly the pertinence escaped him.

"Holland," said Arcane.

"How do you know?"

"I am Arcane."

"That's for damned sure."

"He is in the area. I want his head."

"You mean you want us to kill him?"

"No," said Arcane with forced patience. "I mean precisely what I say. I want his head. Frozen, in a special subzero unit I will provide you. The rest of him, dispose of. Now go."

"Yes, sir," he said, tossing off an exaggerated salute.

Abigail went to the window and watched Arcane's troops deploying themselves, heading out in truck after truck. It was confusing to her . . . as confusing as the bizarre dreams she'd had the night before. Only the faintest traces of them remained, and that same name . . . a name that, curiously, gave her a sense of inner peace. She repeated it to herself over and over in the course of the day, like a mantra. She drew strength from it. The strength that, she hoped, would enable her to deal with her stepfather.

There are humans . . . scurrying about like ants . . . this day. I wonder what they want . . . but it is of no concern.

The woman . . . whose soul I felt in the night . . . I cannot stop thinking . . . of her. Earth mother . . . what is she to me . . . ?

If I am of the earth . . . as was Adam . . . is she my Eve . . . in this fruitful garden? Will I lie naked with her . . . my soul exposed to her . . . ?

Can I trust her . . . for she is only human . . . and I am so much more . . .

. . . and so much . . . less.

Deep in the green, the Swamp Thing gave no heed as Arcane's troops tromped through the brush. They hadn't the faintest idea of what they were looking for except to be concerned since, at any given moment it appeared, the vegetation might turn on them.

Not surprisingly they found nothing despite an entire day of searching. One security man, Conklin, was busy staring at the trees, and before he knew it he was up to his ass in quicksand. Fortunately he was rescued from this ignominious fate. (Unfortunately he was destined for a far more ignominious fate, so this was a mixed blessing at best.)

Night had fallen, and surprisingly the skies had yielded no further rain that day.

At the bottom of the mansion's central stairway, Arcane stood waiting, immaculately dressed in a white dinner jacket.

Abby appeared at the top of the stairs and hesitated. Looking down, she had a dizzying, uncomfortable association she did not like at all. She closed her eyes a moment to compose herself and then forced a smile and walked slowly down the steps. She was freshly coiffed, stylishly dressed in an attractive green gown with matching gloves she hoped hid her tightening knuckles.

She stepped off the bottom step, breathing an inward sigh of relief as Arcane said, "Formally dressed for dinner. How fun."

"Yes, indeedy," said Abby with false cheer. "Puttin' on the Ritz."

He extended an arm, and after only the briefest of hesitations she took it. They walked slowly down the hall toward the main dining room.

"After all these years I never thought I would ever see you again. Perhaps this visit will bring us close. Very close."

He sounded so polished, so suave. There didn't seem to be the slightest hint of the sinister about him. Indeed, when she looked back on her visit thus far, she had been the unpleasant one. As if she were reacting to something imagined. Uncertain, she gave a tentative smile.

At the doorway to the dining room, that creepy guard Arcane had called Gunn was standing there. He looked like he'd been trekking through the swamp all day, and he was lovingly stroking an M16 in a most unsettling manner.

He stared at Abby in that way he had earlier and then turned to Arcane and said, "Doc, just thought you should know, we haven't found anything yet."

"It doesn't matter," replied Arcane calmly.

"What's going on?" Abby asked.

"Nothing. A group of hitchhikers got lost. I volunteered my people to find them. No luck, I'm afraid." The answer was very smooth. Too smooth, her mind warned her.

They went on past Gunn, and she could feel his gaze still on her. A chill cut through her. Just being near him made her feel unclean.

The spread that had been laid out was most impressive. Arcane, at his end of the long, elegant dining room table, was meticulously dissecting the drumstick of a roast duck. Abby poked at her potato without much enthusiasm, not touching any meat. To Arcane's left was Lana, clad in a clinging gold lamé dress. She looked impassive but stared at Abby with burning . . . what? Resentment? Fear? What was it? To Arcane's right was Rochelle, who merely watched Abby with that same detached air he always had.

Abby got the distinct impression she should be between two pieces of glass on a microscope. Perhaps she already was.

"So, Abigail," said Arcane cheerily. "Tell me about yourself. What have you been doing these last ten years."

"Gee, that's funny," answered Abby, unconsciously imitating Arcane's jovial manner. "I was going to ask you the same thing."

Arcane stared at her for a moment. Then he put down his fork, the creases in his face deepening. "I'll be blunt. Why this unexpected visit?"

So there it was. After the better part of an hour engaged in meaningless banter, commenting endlessly on the quality of the food, there it was in the open. Still, she speculated, it was surprising candor from a man she believed to be a master of prevarication.

She held onto the fork, as if holding a sharp instrument in her hand gave her a measure of security. "I guess you could call this an exorcism," she said after a time.

The idea seemed to intrigue him. "And how is that?"

"I seem to be haunted by things I can't resolve . . . feelings about you, about my mother, about her . . . death." She paused, mustering her main assault. "Why was there no funeral?"

He sighed. "We went through all this before. She wanted to be cremated without ceremony."

An image flashed in her mind, unbidden, her mother cold as death, with blue skin and her white-blond ringlets of hair now delicate curls of ice. . . .

She shook it off with effort as she said, "My mother loved me. I was her only child. She would have wanted me there; I know it."

Arcane sighed, putting on the air (or was it genuine) of a patient but tired father. He got up and moved to a cabinet, picking up a beautifully framed photo of Abby's mother. "Abigail, I loved your mother very much. I was lost after she died. I didn't contact you because . . . well, it was always very clear that you didn't approve of my marriage to your mother."

"And you were, what, punishing me somehow?" she demanded.

And Lana, who had been silent until that time, now blurted out, "What do you want from him? You twist everything! He cared for her! And for you!"

"More than he does for you? Is that it?" shot back Abby.

Arcane interposed himself between the two, putting up his hands pleadingly. "Let us put this all behind us. I want us to be friends. Good friends."

He paused, looking from one to the other, and then said softly, "Lana . . . there's a small box in the top right-hand drawer of the desk in my bedroom. Would you bring it back down to me, please?"

She bit off a response, and it was clear to Abby that Arcane was trying to put some distance between the two women. But was it to prevent further fights? Or was it because he was concerned Lana might say something she should not?

As Lana left, Abby said, "This small box she's getting . . . is this your way of buying me off?"

He looked repelled. "Buy off? What an ugly expression. It's something very precious, and I want you to have it."

The silent Rochelle was looking from one to the other as if watching a tennis match. He was able to give his neck a rest now, however, for a silence hung over the dining room. Both Abby and Arcane seemed determined to look everywhere but at each other.

Moments later Lana returned, setting the small box down in front of Abby. Abby stared at it, running a finger across the finely carved wood. It seemed to be in the intricate shape of a tree. She couldn't help but smile, and she said sincerely, "It's beautiful."

"Open it," he prompted.

Slowly she raised the lid and gasped. A large diamond ring glittered from within, its facets shining with inner fire.

"It belonged to your mother," said Arcane quietly. "Just as I know her wish would have been for you not to inflict the raw emotional wound on yourself that attending her funeral would have been, I know she would have wanted you to have this ring."

She removed the ring, studied it, and admired its beauty, and then slid it on her finger. "I hope this doesn't mean we're engaged," she said with a light laugh. It was the first moment of humor she'd felt since she'd come there.

And then she gave a small yelp.

From directly beneath the setting, blood began to flow freely. Something sharp had dug into the fleshy portion of her finger as she'd slid the ring on.

Immediately there was a flurry of activity. As Arcane apologized profusely, Rochelle stepped in quickly, holding a clean cloth against the wound.

And Abby felt something under the cloth. Something plastic.

She stood quickly, knocking aside the cloth.

To her astonishment she saw that Rochelle was palming a small vial. A small amount of the blood had been soaked up by the cloth, but the majority was in the vial.

"What're you, *nuts?!*" she shouted, pulling away her hand and wrapping a cloth around it.

"I was . . . I was just . . . just . . ." Rochelle began to stammer helplessly, looking to Lana for support.

And Lana, stepping in smoothly, said, "You know, Dr. Rochelle was mentioning earlier that you didn't look quite well. Actually slightly anemic. You know how men of medicine are. Once he saw that you were bleeding anyway, he just—"

"Just *happened* to have a test tube on him?" Abby said incredulously. "That's sick! You people are sick!" She backed away from them. "And you're the head sick-o!" She stabbed a finger at Arcane.

He gestured helplessly. "My dear, I had nothing to do with this! I merely wanted to give you this gift." He pointed to the blood-encrusted ring Abby had thrown to the ground.

"Right! Like you gave it to my mother," snapped Abby. She headed for the door.

"Where are you going?" he asked, in a voice filled with concern.

"Out! Don't wait up!"

The door slammed behind her.

Out by the front gate, Points and Conklin were playing a bizarre form of mumblety-peg, with a machete, throwing it at each other's feet.

"Getting dark," said Conklin nervously.

"Don't worry," replied Points. "Enough light from Gunn's cigarette."

She chucked a finger at Gunn, who was leaning against the fence, sharpening his knife against a rock.

He dropped the rock, however, and his hand went toward his gun as he heard quick steps approaching the gate, coming from the direction of the mansion. The other guards also assumed ready positions, but they all relaxed when Abby came into view.

"Excuse me, Miss Arcane," he said as Abby got within distance. "Where are you going?"

"Out."

He took a long, thoughtful drag on his cigarette

as Conklin spoke up, saying, "The swamp is dangerous at night."

"So's the dining room. I'll take my chances."

Gunn surveyed her for a moment, then picked up his walkie-talkie and said slowly, "Doc? Your lovely stepdaughter's here. Wants to go for an evening stroll. Wouldn't suggest it."

In the dining room Arcane's finger hovered over the intercom, considering what to say in response. The easiest thing would be to hold her there.

But he had an instinct, something bothering him in the back of his mind. Then it came to him, a name, shouted by his stepdaughter in the night that he had at first heard and then thought he had imagined.

Alec, she had called. Alec. But he knew only one Alec.

He looked out through the dining room window, out at the swamp beckoning beyond the perimeter.

His place . . .

Alec, had been the cry. Was it possible . . . ?

All this went through his mind in only a moment and then he depressed the talk button and said crisply, "Abigail is not a prisoner here. If you have warned her of the risk, she is certainly free to come and go as she pleases."

At the other end he heard Gunn's surprised voice say, "Okay; you're the doctor."

Arcane nodded and clicked off as he turned toward the questioning Lana, Rochelle having already disappeared into the bowels of the laboratory.

"We may need her," Lana said, as close to disapproving as she ever got with Arcane. "If her blood is the same as her mother's . . . well, she shouldn't be allowed to run around in the swamp at night unescorted. It's crazy."

He smiled mirthlessly. "Sanity is an accusation that has never been leveled at me," he said.

Gunn's voice crackled back on. "She's gone, Doc. Off into the swamp."

"Follow her. Keep me apprised, and make no move without my direct order. Keep a far distance."

"On it."

He turned back to Lana and said, "Have no concern. I don't believe she will be unescorted. As strange as it may sound . . . I believe she's going on a date."

10

In the darkness of the swamp, an area was lit up by two fires, one next to the other.

The first was the roaring power source that kept the still brewing its moonshine. The second was the smaller campfire that a beefy, well-muscled man named Gurdell was hunched in front of. The cuffs of his unwashed jeans were frayed, and his large beer belly (suggesting he had imbibed as much of his hooch as he had sold) hung over the unbuttoned tops. In addition he had striped suspenders, and a baseball cap worn backward like a catcher's.

Gurdell swigged down another draft of the hooch as nearby his brother Clyde checked to make sure the still was operating smoothly. Clyde was thin where Gurdell was fat, blond where Gurdell was dark-haired, nervous where Gurdell was loudly confident, and stupid where Gurdell was . . . well, stupid, really.

He ambled back to the fire. "Great batch o' shine, eh, Gurdell?" he said eagerly.

"Best this month, Clyde. What we gonna do fer fun tonight?"

It was a question Clyde always dreaded, for it meant using imagination, something in which he was in short supply. "Feel like stealin' a car?"

"Nah."

"How about we burn down a house?"

"Nah."

"Hey, how 'bout," and he drew closer, "how 'bout we drive to the motel and run over some dogs."

"I'm sick of runnin' over dogs—'sides, that motel is spooked."

"Well . . ."—Clyde sighed in exasperation—"what you feel like doin', then? My brain's gettin' tired comin' up with all these ideas."

Gurdell pondered that. "I feel like killin' somethin'," he said at length.

"You always feel like killin' somethin'."

That brought a coarse laugh. "Maybe I'll kill you."

Clyde picked up his own bottle. "I'll kill you back with my dyin' breath."

"Your breath's so bad, you might just do it." He laughed again.

"Gurdell," said Clyde impatiently, "it's time we went to town and got us a woman."

Gurdell blinked at that. Damn, it had been a long time. Things seem to crawl to a halt in the swamp.

"I don't recall what one looks like," he said in wonderment.

And the gods, in their infinite jest, decided to give Gurdell a visual aid.

Abby, waterlogged, gown soiled, stumbled into the clearing.

They gaped at her in open astonishment. The timing alone was enough to affirm belief in a supreme being—provided you believed in a supreme being who would give a gorgeous woman . . . *any* woman . . . to two utter scuzzballs as a plaything.

Clyde and Gurdell chose to believe.

"Hi, guys," said Abby, who had been tromping around for so long that Arcane and Lana with their significant looks, and Rochelle with his little vials, were starting to look pretty good. "You wouldn't happen to know which way back to the Arcane place, would you?"

Gurdell approached her. "You talk funny. Where you from?"

"Uh . . . California."

"I hate California." He came closer.

Backing up slowly, Abby shrugged. "Hey, I'll move. Nooo problem."

And now Clyde was shoulder-to-shoulder with his brother. "Anybody know you're out here?"

"Oh, sure . . . the FBI. Charles Bronson. The Rams defensive line . . ."

"You're real pretty."

"Not really," she said quickly, trying to find a way out. "Actually I'm dark and swarthy. Like

Dukakis. My parents were Greek immigrants. This is all makeup."

"She's from California," Gurdell spat out.

"I like her," said Clyde.

"I hate her."

"Okay," said Clyde reasonably. "I'll grab her, and you kill her."

"Okay."

"Then we'll go run over some dogs."

Gurdell grinned a toothless smile. "Yeah."

She turned to run and Clyde leapt, throwing himself onto her back and driving her down. She clawed at the dirt and struggled as she felt Gurdell grabbing at her, touching her.

A name screamed through her mind and she tried to speak it, but she couldn't as Clyde pressed his foul mouth against hers.

She couldn't speak the name.

It didn't matter.

The earth erupted around them.

Clyde and Gurdell coughed violently, dust up their nose and in their eyes, and Gurdell staggered to his feet, trying to pull himself together.

He stopped, rubbed his eyes, stopped again.

A massive creature was standing there, with burning red eyes and a body covered with moss and muck.

"Damn! This guy's dirtier'n you, Clyde!" said Gurdell in shock.

Abby looked up from the ground. Her eyes widened.

"What in hell are you supposed to be?" demanded Gurdell, the shock giving way to amazement.

And Abby whispered, "Alec . . ."

He turned his gaze on her, and nodded slowly.

Her voice choked in her throat, the oppressive nearness of the offensive Clyde forgotten. "Oh, God . . . I'm not losing my mind. . . . It's you . . ."

There was the ugly *click clack* of a shotgun round being chambered.

Gurdell had pulled out his weapon from behind the logs they'd been sitting on, and he said dangerously, "One more time . . . who are you?"

He stared at them for a moment, and if they'd had any brains at all, they would have been terrified by what they saw there. "I am . . . Swamp Thing."

"Right, right." He took aim. "And I'm Bird Shit."

His finger tightened on the trigger, and Abby screamed as a blast roared, echoing through the bog. The shot ripped into Swamp Thing's chest. Gurdell fired again and blew away some more.

He stopped, lowering his rifle in shock.

Swamp Thing was advancing on him, ripped away portions of his anatomy already regenerating. In three great steps he was upon Gurdell, and he tore the gun from Gurdell's hands and bent it in half.

Clyde, from nearby, screeched, leaping away from Abby as if she'd grown horns. Gurdell backed up desperately and tripped over one of the massive logs that had lain there for who knew how long. Swamp Thing stood over him, glowering, and then reached down and effortlessly lifted the log.

He swung it around, almost taking off Clyde's head, the latter diving down out of the way. Gurdell, from his vantage, saw what the intended target was. "Not the still!" he howled.

The huge log smashed into the still. There was an earsplitting crunch of metal as Swamp Thing completely demolished the machine, and when the now-unleashed fire threatened to spread, the earth seemed to come alive. The ground beneath the fire opened up, smothering the flame, and an underground spring burbled up, extinguishing whatever trace bits of the fire might have escaped.

He turned on them then, and, holding high the log, he rumbled in his sepulchral voice, "This is . . . the corpse of a tree . . . and I will use it . . . to make human corpses . . . if I must."

He began to swing it once again, and it was all the urging the two rednecks needed. With panicked screams they bolted toward the bushes. Clyde was not quite fast enough as the tail end of the swinging log caught him and sent him flying into a patch of prickers. There was a most satisfying scream, followed by a string of profanity, much rustling, and eventually, silence.

The Swamp Thing, easily holding a log that a dozen strong men would have had trouble lifting, looked down upon the terrified woman.

"You should not . . . be out at night," he said. "There are . . . monsters everywhere. . . ."

"Up . . ." she paused, trying to force words from her throat. "Up until now . . . I thought monsters were only in people's minds."

"People . . . are the worst kind . . . of monsters."

Clyde and Gurdell crashed noisily through the swamp as if the hordes of hell were right behind them.

For the first five minutes of their headlong plunge they had been screaming and shouting. Now they were conserving their breath and just running like madmen. Forgotten was the still, and the confusion about what they should do tonight. Uppermost in their minds was putting as much distance between themselves and the Swamp Thing as possible.

He was lurking everywhere. Every branch they banged into, every creeper or root that reached out and snagged their feet, every pricker bush that ripped their clothing and tore their skin, most certainly had to be the enraged swamp creature lashing out at them. He was punishing them for their belligerence, letting them know that no matter how fast and how far they ran, he would be there to terrify them.

They burst out of cover and spotted a small structure some yards off. It was the motel, the one Gurdell had been certain was spooked. Now it seemed like an island of sanity, and they dashed for it.

The knob to the screen door came off in Clyde's frantic hand, and a voice from inside said "Knob come off again?" but it barely slowed them down as they smashed right through the screen door.

There was some hippie freak behind the front desk, and a burned-out–looking guy in the corner, staring into empty space.

"Well, now," said the desk clerk, "you look like a couple of sinister ducks. What's your problem, hey?"

"There was a creature! In the swamp!" howled Gurdell. "Y'gotta call somebody!"

"It tried to kill us!" affirmed Clyde.

The man in the corner looked up with a flickering of interest. He looked at the two frantic brothers, at the dozens of cuts and bruises, at the ripped clothes and desperate air. "Creature?" he said.

"It said it was a Swamp Thing! But it was the devil!" Gurdell said, going quickly toward the man in the corner. He grabbed him by the shoulders, desperation in his face. "The swamp's haunted! We can't ever go back or he'll kill us!"

"What's he done so far?"

"So far! He beat us up! He laughed off point-blank shotgun blasts! He picked up a log that weighed half a ton and trashed our still!"

"Your still?"

"That's right," said Clyde. "I'm Clyde; this is Gurdell. We make . . . made . . . hooch."

The man nodded slowly, a smile beginning to crawl across his face tentatively, as if entering unfamiliar territory. For the first time in what seemed ages, he felt life entering his body. "Don't worry," he said. "I know what to do."

"You do!" exclaimed Gurdell, overjoyed.

"Yes." He pulled his service revolver out from under his jacket and flashed his badge. "Harry Dugan, Treasury Department. You're both under arrest for illegally operating a still."

"Wh . . . what?" stammered Clyde.

From behind the desk, Alan said, " 'Fraid so, gents. He's a fed. Chances are you're both going to be guests of the government in some prison far away."

"Far away?" echoed Gurdell.

They looked at each other, then at Dugan.

They dropped to their knees and embraced him fervently.

"Thank you!" they howled. "Thank you thank you thank you."

And with a grateful sob, Clyde said, "I knew it. I knew there was a God all along."

11

She ran a tentative finger across his mossy chest where the bullets had come and gone. There was no trace. "Are you sure you're all right?"

Tenderly he caressed her face. "Now. Yes."

"Who are you?"

"I am . . . Swamp Thing. I was . . . Alec Holland." He paused, still not able to believe she was standing there. She was trembling slightly. "And you . . . ?"

"Abby Arcane."

His face seemed to darken, like a thundercloud. "You are . . . his daughter?"

"He's my stepfather," she said quickly, with the distinct feeling she'd just stepped into something unpleasant.

"Stepfather . . . yet you use . . . his name?"

"Well, when my mother married him, she got him to formally adopt me. It was her way of trying to make us a real family. Yeah, sure." She laughed unpleasantly. "Like the Munsters. Besides, it used to be Abigail Flooglehoff, and anything's better than that." She paused. "You know him, don't you."

"I know him."

"That sounds like an indictment."

He looked down at the hand that was resting against his chest, and saw the dried blood on her fingers. "Did those men . . . hurt you . . . ?"

"Huh? Oh, no, this is from dinner."

"I do not . . . understand."

She shook her head. "Believe me, neither do I."

"Perhaps . . . I can help."

He reached down for her hand . . .

And reflexively she pulled away. Immediately she hated herself for it. Somehow, in some way, she had touched the soul of this monstrous creature before her, yet something within her had made her flinch, purely because of his appearance.

And she'd hurt him. She could see the sadness mirrored in his eyes. "I'm sorry . . ." he rumbled. "Sometimes I forget . . . what I look like."

He spoke so slowly, as if he carried the age of the world on his shoulders. Which, she realized, perhaps he did. Still, it was an incredible concept for her to fathom. "This is all you?" she asked. "For real? I don't understand." She made a vague, helpless gesture. "How could this be?"

"If I tell you . . . about Arcane . . . you will understand."

Suddenly Abby became aware of the ground stirring behind her. She spun and saw something large and leafy emerging from the earth. The plant grew several feet high, vines twisting through it to give it strength and support, and within moments a perfectly serviceable chair had come into existence behind her.

He gestured toward it. "Please."

Incredulously she sat, feeling like the queen of the swamp. Swamp Thing . . . Alec, she reminded herself . . . did not sit, but towered over her, impressive and majestic.

"I was . . . a scientist . . . working in a laboratory . . . not far from here," he said. "My sister . . ." He paused, as if pulling up a distant and treasured memory. "My sister," he continued, his voice sounding softer, ". . . and I had discovered . . . a biorestorative formula . . . that could double the world's . . . food production. Arcane . . . discovered our plan. . . ."

It came roaring back at him, the pain and horror. "He murdered my sister . . . and when he tried to steal the formula . . . I was caught . . . in a terrible explosion. . . ."

"Oh, God," she whispered.

"The flames . . . consumed my body . . . but somehow . . . the chemicals in the formula . . . reconstructed my tissue . . . from the swamp . . . and I became . . . what you see."

"You mean my stepfather . . . is responsible for your being like this?"

Again he nodded slowly. "Yes . . . and he found me . . . and I killed him."

"But . . . but you didn't. I mean, I just had dinner with him."

Swamp Thing actually seemed startled. "I *thought* I had. It appears from my existence . . . and his . . . that nothing dies easily . . . in the swamp . . . Abby." He actually spoke with urgency: "Arcane . . . is evil . . . in its purest form . . . and you must leave immediately."

"I can't!" Abby pleaded. "My mother is dead, and they know what happened to her. It's like some private, sick joke of theirs, and I have to find out what it was."

He studied her for a long moment. "If she is dead . . . then she is beyond your help . . . and risking your own life . . . will do her no good."

"People have risked their lives for knowledge plenty of times, Alec."

He paused and then actually whispered, in a tone touchingly human, " 'Alec' . . . how long it has been . . . since I heard that name . . . as inappropriate . . . as that might be." He shook off the thought. "Yes . . . they have risked their lives . . . for knowledge . . . that would be of benefit . . . to others. No one will benefit . . . from your risks."

"I will."

"Then you are . . . being selfish with your life."

"Alec," she moaned, "you don't . . ."

"Understand?" He shook his head. "Who could understand . . . better than I?"

"I know, but—"

"If you saw the world . . . as I do . . . you would realize . . . that your concepts of life and death

. . . do not begin to grasp . . . the whole. Life is death . . . and death is life . . . and to become obsessed . . . to the point of exclusion with one . . . is to misunderstand the need . . . for the other."

She gazed into his eyes and saw things in there, emotions and comprehensions of a grand scheme of things she could only discern the barest glimmerings of.

All her life she had been certain there was more to the world than she had been permitted to see or understand. Her affairs with men had been transitory and unfulfilling. Her relationship—if one could call it that—with nature was longstanding yet requited only as much as her imagination would allow it to be.

Here was the key to understanding, the key to something within her that had been crying to get out from the moment of her birth.

Here was Alec.

"All right," she said quietly. "All right, I . . . I can't forget what I came here to do. But . . . I won't go back just yet. Let's . . . let's just go someplace and talk."

A place . . . yes, a place . . . where she can be comfortable . . . and at ease.

Humans have homes . . . but my home . . . is all that I am. In order for her to be at peace . . . there must be . . . some touchstone of her reality.

Just as I . . . have fashioned a body . . . approximating a human's . . . so must I create a home

. . . I can bring her to . . . where she will be . . . at ease.

I reach out . . . searching for someplace . . . that will be an easy walk . . . and I find a large tree . . . in a clearing . . . with great, sturdy branches . . . and hollowed-out areas . . . where animals found shelter. . . . But it is old . . . and dying . . . and inappropriate . . . in its current state . . .

But not . . . unsalvageable. . . .

"Yes . . ." he said slowly. "There is . . . a place. Walk this way."

Abby put an imaginary cigar to her mouth and, doing a poor Groucho Marx impression, said, "If I could walk that way, I wouldn't need the talcum powder."

He stared at her and, if he had had eyebrows, they would have been furrowed.

"Joke." She gestured helplessly. "Just a kind of stupid joke. I guess, after getting burned up and dumped in a swamp and turning green and spongy, you wouldn't have much of a sense of humor."

"Actually . . . I had very little . . . before." Somewhere under the mass of leaves and muck were the beginnings of a smile. "But . . . for you . . . I shall make . . . the effort."

Gunn whistled and lowered the binoculars. The squad of security guards around him whispered, "What? What do you see?"

For answer he lifted his walkie-talkie. "Doc," he said slowly. "She's with him."

Points and Conklin looked at each other in confusion, as did all the others.

Arcane's voice came back: "You're certain it's him?"

With a sneer Gunn replied, "Well, from this distance it's hard to be sure. It could be John Forsythe. *Yes,* I'm certain it's him. Do we attack?"

"Not yet." There was a pause. "Pull back. Keep them under observation. But do nothing overtly hostile to them. To anything, for that matter. He's very sensitive."

"Oh, right, we wouldn't want to make him cry."

"That's not what I mean" came Arcane's voice with an edge that could have cut Gunn to ribbons had he been present. "He's preternaturally aware of the environment. Hostile maneuvers, something as innocuous as gutting a raccoon for fun, might catch his attention. The longer he is with Abby, the more he will become distracted, and the better our chances are of surprising him."

"Well, hell, why don't we wait to see if they hit the sack together and grab 'em while they're smoking some goddamn cigarettes?"

"You think you are joking, Gunn. Do not underestimate his capabilities."

"Well, fine, Doc," said Gunn with thinning patience. "You're the big expert; why don't you come out here and handle it personally?"

There was a pause, and then Arcane spoke. "I

have every confidence in you, Gunn. Wait until you think the moment is right, then strike. Arcane out."

Gunn sat there, staring at the walkie-talkie, and then he grinned. "He's afraid."

"Bullshit," said Points. "You don't know what you're talkin' about, Gunn, which is hardly anything new."

"He's chickenshit scared, I tell ya," replied Gunn, taking a drag on his cigarette. "That walking Spinach Soufflé out there has the great Anton Arcane spooked. Well, fine . . . let's wait awhile."

Points took the binoculars from Gunn and focused on them. Her mouth dropped open. "She's resting her head on his arm! That's sick!"

"Hey, they always say all the good men are either married or gay." Gunn snickered. "That guy is neither. He's just a vegetable . . . but that shouldn't get in the way of true love. Why, hell, there's only one thing Miss Arcane there needs to make this romance work."

"And that is?" prompted Conklin.

Gunn snickered. "Thousand Island dressing."

Arcane stood in the center of his bedroom in a dark mood. He had come up to take the bath he always took at this time, but the shortwave conversation with Gunn had discomfited him.

"Lana?" he called out, but there was no answer. He went to the window, stared out at the swamp once more.

There, at the edge of the fence, was where Arcane's dominion ended. It was unfair, unjust. His was the superior mind, the greater ambition. Why was it that, through an accident, Holland had all the green beyond, and immortality, and Arcane had to fight and battle to hold on to what precious little he had? Arcane had a bleak, limiting future, and Holland had an infinity of tomorrows. . . .

Tomorrow and tomorrow and tomorrow . . .

He whispered, " 'A tale told by an idiot, full of sound and fury, signifying nothing.' "

"Dr. Arcane?"

He became dimly aware of Rochelle calling him for long moments now. He turned slowly.

Rochelle hovered in the shadow of the doorway. "If I may be candid, sir, you seem very far away."

Arcane smiled thinly. "Strangely enough, I was having a conversation with Macbeth."

"Macbeth?" Rochelle shook his head uncomprehendingly.

"Yes, the doomed soul. I am a doomed soul. Two doomed souls conversing. Do you know what you have when you have two doomed souls?"

"Doomed shoes?" offered Rochelle.

Arcane did not so much as crack a smile, and Rochelle shifted uncomfortably. "What do you want, Rochelle?"

"Please forgive the intrusion, sir . . ."—Rochelle waved some notes he was carrying nervously—"but I must speak with you. It's very important."

"Get on with it."

"Well . . . I hate to put it this way, it's so trite, but . . . there's good news and bad news. The bad news is the blood tests I ran on you twenty-four hours ago have been completed, and . . . I'm afraid the deterioration has increased."

"You mean I'm in danger of reverting to that . . . that grotesque animalistic form." He closed his eyes as if to block the sight from his mind.

"Worse. Complete cellular breakdown. You'll . . . you'll virtually crumple into nothing unless the process is reversed."

Arcane stared at the backs of his hands, where the cracking, drying skin could no longer be denied. "The good news," he said softly, "had better be damned good."

"We've found, in the blood sample we got from your stepdaughter, the same type of antigen that existed in the blood of your late wife."

Arcane looked up with renewed hope.

"But if we don't act within the next seventy-two hours, the deterioration may become permanently irreversible," warned Rochelle.

"And this antigen . . . could it possibly provoke a fatal immune reaction?"

Rochelle nodded, flinching as if afraid Arcane would strike him. "I'm afraid so, unless we can obtain a counteragent from a subject with a compatible blood type."

"And genetically splice the two," Arcane said slowly.

"Exactly. However, because of the large amounts of blood required, the process would doubtless be fatal to the donor, and there are only two persons on staff with the correct blood type. The security man, Conklin, and . . . uh . . . Dr. Zurrell."

Arcane did not hesitate a moment. "Check Conklin's whereabouts. If he's out with Gunn, arrange for one of the men here to relieve him, and say he's required to assist you in the lab. If Conklin should die before you have the full amount of blood required, then," and he shrugged, "although I would hate to lose Lana . . . do whatever is necessary. Clear?"

"Yes, sir, but . . . may I ask you a candid question?"

Arcane waited for it, certain it was regarding the morality of using Dr. Zurrell.

He should have known better as Rochelle asked, "Have you given any thought to that salary increase we spoke about . . . ?"

"Your question is too candid," said Arcane tightly, and he stalked out of the room, all thoughts of his bath erased by the whirl of the preparation that would have to be made as their timetable had been unexpectedly moved up. Abby would definitely be brought back, but everything had to be ready before that. There was so much to be done, and where the devil had Lana gone off to?

The answer to that had been in Arcane's own bathroom. Lana was sitting there on the floor, wrapped only in a towel, her knees pulled up to her face, rocking back and forth gently and sobbing. Nearby her the bath was filled with water that was rapidly going from hot to tepid.

She had wanted to surprise him, have the bath ready and herself waiting in it for him.

She had been in the bathroom and had heard every word Arcane and Rochelle had said.

Every damned word.

12

They walked slowly through the swamp, and Abby could feel the life all around them, watching them, fascinated. The coolness of him felt marvelous against her. "So where's this place we're going to? Is it your home? How long have you lived there?"

"Actually . . . it is . . . under construction."

"When will it be finished?"

"Shortly before we arrive."

"Oh." She paused. "Is there a . . . y'know . . . Mrs. Swamp Thing?"

"No . . . I am a . . . bachelor."

"Yeah, well, you scientific types . . . your work is your life, I guess."

"Literally."

They stepped into the clearing, and Abby gasped in astonishment.

The trees seemed to caress the heavens. Great leaves stretched forth, which would provide shade in the daytime and shelter from rain at night. The trunk was twice as wide as Abby, with a large hole serving as a door. When she stepped through, to her shock, she found a stairway hewn out of the living wood itself. She followed it upward, peering into great chambers filled with the softest moss. The entire place smelled of the beauty and simplicity of nature. It was intoxicating.

She picked a chamber at random and walked in, having to bend only slightly, and still having trouble coping with the fact that she was in a tree. She eased herself down carefully onto the moss floor and felt the first cool breeze she had detected since coming to the swamp in the first place. Behind her was a wall of wood, but it was open in front of her, and she looked out, surveying the swamp from her unique vantage.

She had to be thirty, maybe forty, feet in the air. It was difficult to make out much of the swamp in the darkness, but far, far in the distance she could glimpse the lights of the Arcane mansion.

She felt an inner revulsion she hadn't before. For some reason, the intrusion of humanity into this place of beauty seemed an abomination.

She heard the Swamp Thing stirring behind her, peering through the chamber "door" from inside the tree trunk, and she tried to find something to say. The entire structure was so outside her frame of reference all she could come up with was "The rent on this place must be incredible. I bet you must earn a lot of the . . ." She paused and realized there was no other way to conclude the sentence. "Green stuff," she finished weakly.

There was an odd sound then from deep in the Swamp Thing's chest, almost like a wheezing or the creaking of a tree.

"It has been a long time . . . since I have laughed," he said.

Is that what it was? I thought it was a freight train on Valium. "Well, I have that effect on most of my boyfriends," she said easily.

"Me . . . your boyfriend?" She heard bemusement in his voice.

"Why not?" she demanded.

He pulled himself up into the chamber with her.

"Abby . . . I have not lost my humanity . . . so long ago . . . that I have forgotten . . . all that is part of it."

"Yeah? So?"

"There are . . . obvious limits. I cannot give you . . . physical love. After all . . . I am a plant."

"That's okay. I'm a vegetarian. Besides, physical love isn't so hot. I mean, once you've done it four or five hundred times, it loses its mystery. At least, that's what I hear," she said quickly, then added, "Anyway, I didn't know I was offering it. Isn't that just like a man—there's any sign of intimacy and—"

"Abby . . . I know why . . . you are saying these things . . . but glib talk . . . cannot begin to hide . . . the differences between us."

She turned toward him then, reached up, and

caressed the side of his head. "I don't want to hide them," she said softly. "I want to cherish them."

"I cannot give you . . . the love you want."

It was incredible to her that there was such fragility in the voice of a being so massively powerful.

She took his hand and said, "Maybe you can give me the love I need."

"You take . . . all I say . . . and turn it . . . to your advantage."

"I'm a woman. That's what we're best at."

"Division of gender . . . and attributes of each . . . are so important to humans."

"Isn't it to everything?"

He reached up, where just over her head was suddenly an orchid. She watched as he brought it in front of her face, passed it slowly just under her nose.

"Humans . . . are by definition . . . half beings," he said slowly. "The man . . . and the woman . . . are each a part of the whole . . . yet eternally separate . . . and alone. That is why . . . physical intimacy is so important . . . to you. It is only during that time . . . that a man and a woman . . . are once again merged . . . into the single entity . . . they are meant to be."

He held up the orchid. "A flower . . . is complete. It has the stamen . . . and the pistil . . . male and female organs . . . together. It is a unit . . . content . . . not endlessly searching . . . for a missing half. Perhaps that is why . . . humans have always envied flowers . . . and tried to destroy them . . . for they are . . . what humans can never be."

She stared at the orchid, then touched it gently. "You're not like the orchid, though," she said softly. "Perhaps you thought you were, but you're starting to realize you're not. Unlike a flower, you're feeling incomplete. You, just like the poor humans, need a companion, a mate."

He nodded slowly. "Nobody is . . . perfect . . . I suppose."

Very gently, very nervously, Abby brought her face around to him. She tried to find his mouth somewhere in the darkness of the lower part of his face, and when she did, she closed her eyes, pictured Tom Selleck in her mind, and kissed him. It was extremely tentative, the merest brushing of lips, and when they parted, she giggled slightly. "Tastes like lime," she said.

They sat there for a time, Abby chewing on her lower lip, Alec thinking of things unknowable. "There isn't any way, though, is there?" she whispered.

He was silent for a bit longer, and then said, "There are ways . . . beyond ways . . . if you are willing. . . ."

In a very small voice, she said, "I'll try anything once."

He paused, seeming to concentrate, and then Abby noticed something beginning to emerge from his chest, just above where his heart would be. It was yellowish brown, like a small potato, or a yam, and when it was halfway out, he reached up and pulled it completely free.

He handed it to her, and uncertainly she held the tuber in her hands and stared at it as if it had just dropped down from outer space. "Uh . . . for me?" she asked. He nodded. "Uh . . . gee, Alec, uhm . . . I'm all for romantic metaphors, with, like, giving me your heart and stuff, but this is a bit much, y'know?"

"It is not . . . my heart . . . although the heart I have created . . . serves no real biological function. . . ."

"No?"

"No . . . the tuber . . . is merely a portion . . . of myself . . . that will enable you . . . to see the world . . . as I do . . . and share yourself . . . with me. . . ."

"Well, hey, okay." She forced a confused smile. Gingerly she held it up to her cheek and looked around, trying to imagine what in God's name Alec was expecting. Not wanting to disappoint him, she said, "Oh, yeah, hey, I see it. It looks, like, really great. What a beautiful world!"

In the darkness of his lower face a smile emerged. "Take a bite."

She stared at the tuber. "You're kidding."

"If you would . . . rather not . . ."

"No, I . . . well, I mean, I just ate a few hours ago. I'm kind of full, and I . . ."

She looked into those unknowable eyes, and wanted to know the mind behind them. The tuber felt so light in her hand.

When she was six years old she'd eaten a worm on a dare. This couldn't possibly be worse than that. Could it?

"Well . . . I mean, I guess just a small bite couldn't hurt, y'know?" Gamely she smiled and raised it to her lips. Talk about your consuming passions, she thought as she nibbled at it.

She chewed it slowly, and it tasted like a sweet potato. Not bad. Not really bad at all. She swallowed it, then leaned back against the Swamp Thing's mossy chest, waiting for something to happen.

Nothing did.

She sighed, not wanting to admit to Alec that she wasn't feeling anything, and then she noticed in a very distant way that her hand was glowing.

"Alec?" she whispered. "Do you see it?"

There was no answer. She held her hand up, staring with rapt attention as shimmering colors radiated outward from her hand, from her arm. All the colors of the rainbow surrounded her, but predominant was red. A soft, joyful glow of life.

It was all over her now, but muted by her clothes. Alec, Arcane, the swamp—everything was secondary to this incredible new sensation. Quickly she peeled off her clothes to see the colors shimmering all over her body. They seemed to stretch outward, to caress the walls of the tree around her, and now that was glowing, too, but a cooler, more peaceful glow, blue mixed with brown.

A bolt of color shot past her, tracing a graceful

arc in the air, like a flashing ember, and she realized to her amazement that it was a mosquito. An insignificant bug, an insect she would have promptly swatted earlier, now was a stunning array of hues and shadings—a blazing light, a symbol of the beauty of life darting just past her eyes.

She looked out upon the swamp, and it was beyond anything she had experienced. A dazzling kaleidoscope, shifting back on itself, shimmering and undulating, blues and greens, and traces of glorious red, small animals wending their way through or sleeping or hunting for food.

She forgot to move. She forgot to think. Abby reached out with her mind, and she was in the plants, and in the animals, and she was the smallest of fish swimming through the water and the highest of birds soaring through the air, and her blood had become as the water and her body had become as the dirt, bristling with life in all its infinite varieties and textures.

She was part of it; it was part of her—the glory and majesty of all there was.

In the rainbow haze around her someone approached her. She saw him, towering and strong, and he was all the colors and more; he was nature's harmony and purity, untampered and unfouled. She felt the barest hint, the slightest taste, of what the world was like when it was new.

The Swamp Thing stood before her, his eyes glistening with joy, and he reached out for her. She had lost all sense of up and down, of time and space. There was Alec, there was she, there was the all, and that was all that mattered. She took his hands, her eyes wide, her lips slightly parted.

Long, tapering vines extended from his arms and encompassed hers. She closed her eyes, feeling the wetness and firmness of the growth, pulsing with God-given life. It surrounded her, moved along her body, tracing the curving slope of her back, the graceful line of her leg. She shivered and trembled, and through half-lidded eyes she looked at Alec.

He was reforming. The moss and green were departing him, leaving behind firm and tanned skin, wood fiber being replaced by human tissue. His eyes lost their redness, became soft and blue as the skies. The deformed shoulders and back smoothed, became smaller and human.

Deep in his chest, his heart began to beat. His lungs expanded and contracted, his chest rising and falling for the first time in what seemed a millennium.

Alec Holland, in the glory of humanity, stood before her. And she . . .

She was an array of flowers. Violets, orchids, roses decorated her—no, grew from her. Her hair was spun straw, her body a breathtaking garden seemingly sculpted from humanity's most ancient memories of Eden.

Their lips joined, and his fingers entangled themselves in the sleek vines of her body as she tenderly stroked the firm flesh of his.

She lay back on a bed of moss, and he was atop

her, their spirits as one and their bodies moments later following suit. Color and heat poured from his skin, from her blades, and for the first time in her life, she was alive.

"What're they up to?"

Gunn was watching through his binoculars, the night already beginning to wane, the dawn mere hours away. He envied Conklin, who'd been recalled for some candy-ass easy assignment back at the mansion. In response to Pointsetta's question, he replied, "Damned if I know. It's so dark over there. There's never any light in a swamp, y'know. They went into some kinda tree, but that was ages ago, and since then I—"

Suddenly there was a rumbling beneath their feet, a quake so powerful it knocked them to the ground, their equipment falling all over the place. The dozen men and women could only stagger about for the long moments until the seizure subsided.

Gunn found himself lying on top of Points. Annoyed, she shoved him off as she sat up and said, "What the hell was that? We never have quakes around here."

"Yeah, I know. It's been ages since I felt the earth move. . . ."

His voice trailed off, and they stared at each other.

"You don't suppose—?" began Points.

They pondered it a moment and then together affirmed, "Naaaah."

13

The first rays of the sun were creeping outward across the swamp, touching the treetops, which seemed to have become hushed with anticipation.

Rochelle was unaware of it. Deep in the pit of the laboratory, he had been working all night, to the point of exhaustion and beyond.

He put down his diagrams and walked across the room, past the unconscious form of security guard Conklin, lying comatose on a diagnostic table with tubes sticking out of what seemed to be every visible portion of his anatomy. He checked the blood flow briefly, then sat down at a nearby table and made himself a glass of Tang, a drink he'd been hooked on ever since the early days of the astronauts.

From the table drawer he pulled out a copy of *Young & Easy* magazine and turned to the centerfold. He studied it with mild interest, and then his eyes widened as he pulled a marker from his jacket pocket and started making sketches on the picture.

"Yes," he said thoughtfully. "She'd definitely look good with fins . . . or maybe flippers. Yes, definitely flippers."

"Doing a little homework, are we, Doctor?" a female voice came from behind him.

Quickly, like a guilty child, he shoved the magazine from sight. "Yes, yes, always thinking of the next experiment."

"You know, I think you work entirely too hard," said Lana. She smiled coldly.

"Well," he began, "excellence is—"

She cut him off, pointing at Conklin. "Isn't that one of the security men?"

"Yes, yes, Conklin, I think his name is. Was." He gestured weakly. "An emergency transfusion for Dr. Arcane."

She studied the unfortunate security guard carefully. "Will he have enough?" she asked very quietly, and with the barest hint of danger in her voice.

She knows! Rochelle's alarmed voice warned him. Then he dismissed the thought. She couldn't know. She was only a woman.

But the blood might not be enough.

But he was lousy at lying.

"There is," and he gathered his thoughts, "there is a good chance his blood will suffice."

"Let's hope so," Lana said in a calm, even tone, then turned and walked out of the lab.

Rochelle let out a breath of air in relief. He had

the distinct feeling he'd just been the victim of a near miss.

A crumpled Ho-Ho wrapper was dropped into the dirt and trod underfoot. Darryl slung the baseball bat over his right shoulder and called out, "Omie?"

Just ahead, Omar was trodding along, loaded down—as was Darryl—with assorted junk foods, sodas, comic books, etc. Instead of a bat, however, he was carrying a camera, which swung loosely on a strap around his neck.

His parents would have a shitfit when they came back tomorrow to discover that his mom's car was a pile of twisted scrap. Fortunately they hadn't seen the newspaper with the article of the previous day's adventures—unsurprising, he supposed, considering his parents had little to no interest in news. Their sole sources of information from the modern world were *USA Today* and *Entertainment Tonight.*

Somehow, even though it wasn't his fault, they'd find a way to blame it on him. He was sure of it. So there was only one thing to do.

Make money. Lots of it, fast. Piles of it; enough to buy a car and more. And there was one sure way to do that.

Get pictures of the Swamp Thing and sell them for a skillion dollars.

Now what the hell was Darryl whining about?

"Omie, I gotta stop!" he moaned, staggering behind his friend.

Without stopping, Omar shot back, "You ain't hungry again, are you?"

"Five minutes!" came the plea. "Five minutes! That's all I ask."

"Last five minutes turned into half an hour. We gotta move." And mercilessly he picked up the pace.

Gunn roused Points and the others from their light doze. "Just daybreak," he whispered. "She's sleepin'. I think he is, too. Let's get 'em."

Within moments the squadron had rubbed the sleep from their eyes, loosened their stiff joints.

They started in the direction of the great tree, which was hundreds of yards away.

Abby slowly stretched, and then lazily brushed away a bug nattering about her face. She felt the moss beneath her naked body and luxuriated in it before slowly sitting up and opening her eyes.

The Swamp Thing was there, seated, his legs drawn up, and he was looking out into the swamp.

Was it all a dream the night before? she wondered. Well, whether it was or it wasn't, it was the kind of dream lives could be built on.

"Alec?" she whispered. Then she smiled shyly. "Do you still respect me?"

He didn't respond at first, then slowly he shook his head.

"You—" Her eyes widened. "You *don't*?"

He turned toward her and seemed to focus on her for the first time. "I . . . am sorry, Abby. I was not . . . paying attention to what . . . you said. What was it?"

"Nothing." She waved it off. "It wasn't important." She drew closer to him. "Something's wrong, though, isn't it?"

"Something . . . in the swamp . . . is stirring. I am not certain yet . . . from where. It will take me a few more moments . . . to locate it. . . ."

"And what will you do when you find it?"

He said darkly, "Whatever I must."

Finally taking pity on his friend, Omar had allowed the two of them to break for a rest, seated on a log. Darryl was digging through their food stash.

"Gimme one of them Ho-Hos, before you eat 'em all," said Omar impatiently.

"Out of Ho-Hos," said Darryl with satisfaction, popping the last one into his mouth.

Omar sighed. "What about Twinkies?"

Darryl stared into the backpack. "Nope."

"Sno-Balls?"

"Nope."

"Ding Dongs?"

"Nope."

"Pudding pies?"

"Nope."

Thoroughly exasperated, Omar almost shouted, "Then what's left?!"

"Got two apples," said Darryl serenely.

"Apples?! Aw, man!"

Suddenly they heard a rustling, a snapping of branches, slow and methodical. "What was that?" whispered Omar.

"I dunno."

"Neither do I. What do you *think* it was?"

"I dunno."

"Neither do I," Omar admitted again.

"Better check it out."

Feeling a sudden decline in nerve, Omar said tersely, "I'm the cameraman. You're the point man. You check it out."

Sounding like a commercial for Life cereal, Darryl promptly fired back, "I'm not checking it out! You check it out!"

"What's the matter, you chicken?" sneered Omar, as if he himself were not.

"Well, I . . ."

"Then check it out, check it out."

Darryl stood slowly, on trembling legs. "What if it gets me?"

"It doesn't want you," Omar reassured. "Nobody wants you."

Darryl paused as he swung his bat experimentally. "My mother wants me," he said defensively.

"Nah. She just keeps you around 'cause if she dumped you somewheres she'd be arrested and stuff. Now get going."

Finding this of cold comfort, Darryl advanced tentatively, probing at the bush with his bat. For two long minutes he poked and prodded, and, finally satisfied, he turned back to his friend saying "You jerk, there's no one . . ."

Omar was completely surrounded by four extremely surly-looking men, one of whom had a gun at the boy's throat.

". . . here." finished Darryl weakly.

"I have something for you," said the Swamp Thing.

They were standing at the base of the great tree house, and Abby, now dressed, said, "Not another one of those psychedelic yams, Alec, please—God, can't you men ever get enough?"

"It is not . . . that," he answered with a sound of amusement. He held a rose out to her, almost shyly.

"I didn't know there were roses in swamps," she said in surprise.

"There are . . . now. Allow me. There are still . . . a few thorns. . . ."

Gently, carefully, he tucked it into her hair. It seemed to hug the side of her head as if happy to have found a home.

"No one's given me flowers since my senior prom. And they were wilted," she recalled.

Suddenly they heard a high-pitched screech for help.

"That . . . that sounds like a child!" said Abby.

"Stay here," he ordered, and ran off into the green.

"Be careful, Alec!" she shouted, which was all

she had time for before she heard the alarming sound of rounds of ammo being chambered from directly behind her.

The largest of the men, a husky former wrestler named Weaver, took a bite out of the apple. "What else you got, kid?" he asked a petrified Omar.

"Got a camera! It's a good one. It's expensive! You can have it!"

"No they can't!" protested Darryl. "It's my dad's!"

"Was your dad's," said Weaver. "Now it's ours."

"So that means you'll let us go, right?" Omar inquired hopefully.

Weaver grinned and glanced at the other guards nearby him. "Wrong," they all chorused.

And from nearby a deep voice corrected them. "Right."

They spun as the Swamp Thing loomed out of the vegetation and advanced on them.

Immediately seeing his chance for fame and glory, Omar swung up the camera and started to click away.

Weaver swung his M16 up and had just enough time to say "Don't move!" before Swamp Thing was upon him. Weaver jammed the gun into Swamp Thing's body and fired. Dirt and mud blew out his back, the spray covering the other guards.

His body reformed around the gun, and the firearm became embedded in it. Swamp Thing half turned at the waist, and the motion yanked the rifle out of Weaver's hands. He tried to lunge after it, but Swamp Thing twisted back the other way and the rifle butt smashed across Weaver's face, knocking out two teeth and breaking his jaw.

Weaver went down, moaning, and the other guards leapt at Swamp Thing, climbing all over him like ants on a hill. He shook them off easily, then grabbed up the agonized Weaver and, using him as a club, battered the remaining guards into insensibility.

That done, one by one he hurled them far off into the brush. He turned slowly toward the wide-eyed Darryl, and then toward Omar who was busily snapping away.

"Are you . . . all right?" he asked.

"Fuh . . . fuh . . . fine," Darryl managed to get out.

His heart pounding, Omar said nonchalantly, "Mind smiling for one more straight-on picture."

"I will try."

He stood there, and his expression did not seem to change all that much. Nevertheless Omar snapped his picture. "Thank you," he said.

"You're welcome. However . . . the lens cap is on."

Omar looked down at the simple black-plastic obstruction that had just cost him a roll of film. He moaned. Then he quickly removed the cap and said again, "Okay, now—"

And from a distance came the scream: *"Alec!"*

Omar took a photograph of empty air, for before the shouted name had faded from the morning dew, Swamp Thing had vanished.

With a deep, heartfelt sigh, Omar thrust the camera at Darryl. "Take the film out," he said, "and chuck it. Then we just gotta keep slogging away and hope we get lucky . . . again."

"You better let me go before your luck runs out!" Abby yelled.

She was fighting Gunn's angry tug every step of the way as he dragged her through the swamp. "Guys, somebody lend me a hand, please!" he said with faltering patience.

One of the larger guards, Hugo, grabbed Abby from behind and unceremoniously tossed her over his shoulder. They started to run once again.

Futilely Abby pounded on his back. "You don't know who you're dealing with!" she shouted. "He'll go crazy when he catches up with you!"

"Where the hell is the airboat?" demanded Gunn. "Which way was it again?"

Tasha pointed with certainty, and they followed her lead, since no one denied that Natasha Pointsetta had the best sense of direction.

Seconds later they got to it, floating serenely and anchored. It was a flat-bottomed boat, powered by an airplane propeller projecting above the stern.

Abby got a brief glimpse of some miscellaneous equipment—guns, rifles, and some other items she didn't recognize—before she was hurled like a sack of potatoes onto the deck. She tried to scramble to her feet, but now Gunn was there, and he stopped her attempts to escape in the most expedient manner—he sat on her.

"Comfy down there?" He grinned.

Points, from the bow of the ship, shouted "Hugo! Cast us off!" From the control board she flicked the ignition, and the huge propeller roared to life.

The roar that came next drowned it out.

"Alec!" shouted Abby, upon hearing it, and with a degree of satisfaction she snapped at Gunn, "You're in deep now, fella."

The Swamp Thing, all his attention focused on Abby, emerged from the reeds, howling his fury and anger at the effrontery of these puny mortals. He lunged toward them, approaching the boat from the rear and getting ready to come around it, to upend it and smash it to pieces.

The boat started to lurch forward, suddenly free of its anchors. One mooring line trailed past him, and Swamp Thing swiftly reached down, snagged it and held onto it tightly. Then, incredibly, hand over hand, he started to draw the powerful airboat toward him.

Points emptied a full clip from her Magnum into him, and he didn't even appear to notice. A deep fear began to build in the pit of her stomach as she realized she was facing something beyond her understanding.

And from the reeds, Hugo, who had been the one to untie the moorings, slammed into Swamp Thing just as he had almost gotten the boat close enough to himself.

With all his strength concentrated on the airboat, Swamp Thing was off balance when the impact from behind came. He staggered forward, fell . . .

. . . and was caught in the massive propeller.

Abby screamed, a high shriek of panic, as the propeller chopped through the muck-encrusted body of Alec Holland.

"That's it!" howled Gunn in celebration. "That's it! Turn him into Mulch Thing!"

From the waist up, Alec was gone, mercilessly shredded by the powerful propeller blade. Hugo grabbed up the Swamp Thing's lower half and tossed that in as well.

"Stop it! Stop it! Oh, God, stop!" Abby shrieked over and over again, unable to so much as move. She struggled furiously against the far greater strength of Gunn and made no headway at all. "You're *killing* him!"

"Nah. Puree, maybe," chortled Gunn.

The propellers were now covered with the ground-up bits of the Swamp Thing. Abby closed her eyes against the grisly sight.

"C'mon, let's go, let's go!" Points called out.

Obediently Hugo leapt onto the airboat, and now the ship roared out into the swamp, hurling itself into the murky waters and plowing through effortlessly.

Abby looked up at Gunn with pure, undiluted hatred. "You bastards."

"I love you, too, honey buns," replied Gunn. "But first thing's first. Gotta get you back to—"

"Look out!"

Hugo's alarmed cry brought Gunn to his feet. Abby tried to jump up as well, but this time Gunn brought the butt of his rifle down on the back of her head. She fell to the deck, barely keeping her consciousness.

Ahead of them, rising from the water like a green ghost, was the Swamp Thing, his body re-forming before their very eyes.

They were thirty yards away and closing, and he was raising his arms above his head and roaring out a challenge.

Gunn's cigarette dropped from his mouth. "Holy shit. How many times do you have to kill that guy?"

Even as Gunn was speaking, Abby saw him grabbing up some sort of tank that was attached to the deck of the ship with metal clips. He cradled the tank in one arm and was swinging around some sort of attached hose with the other.

"Hard right!" he shouted. "Now!"

The airboat swerved to the right, just beyond Swamp Thing's outstretched fingers. He turned on them, his face a picture of fury, and within five seconds would have caught up with them and rended their ship, and them, to bits.

It was five seconds he didn't have, for within two seconds the air was blistered with heat as Gunn unleashed the flame-thrower.

Swamp Thing made a sound Abby had never heard from him before . . . a sound of fear. It was a horrified scream, and she realized it was not Swamp Thing reacting, but Alec Holland.

Swamp Thing needn't have feared fire. Swamp Thing could have simply dived back into the green, created a new body for himself in instants.

But Alec Holland, the reawakened man, was reliving the most terrifying moment, the last moment, of his life.

She had been with him, been a part of him. All that he was was now a part of her, and she felt through her haze the panicked agony he had felt when he'd been caught in the explosion. A man ablaze, a human comet, had come into existence and died that day, all in the space of a few soul-searing moments.

She felt his mind become paralyzed with the fear of the man he had been, the man whose essence she had touched last night. If it had not been for her, he might not have reacted this badly.

Swamp Thing lurched around, the water surrounding his knees becoming clouds of steam. His body was vanishing in a smoking blaze. He howled a name—"Linda,"—and his arms blackened completely and fell away; the moist leaves of his body dried and crispened and crumbled, and within seconds the lifeless carcass of Swamp Thing collapsed into a smoldering pile of leaves and grass.

By that time the airboat was far, far away, and the last thing Abby heard before she allowed herself to lapse into merciful unconsciousness was Gunn's triumphant laugh.

14

Lana Zurrell entered the lab quickly and, with some impatience, spotted Rochelle once again trying to hide away his nonsensical girlie magazines. Not in any mood for more of his absurdity, she got straight to the point. "They've captured the girl. Gunn is bringing her down here. We'd best get Conklin out of sight, so Gunn won't . . ." Her voice trailed off as she looked at the vacant table where Conklin had been. "Where is he?"

"In deep freeze," said Rochelle easily, getting to his feet. "He was near death from the blood loss, so I put him on ice until he recovers. Although it won't be in time for the operation, I fear."

"Wait, wait." Lana shook her head in confusion. "What deep freeze? What are you talking about? I've never seen a deep freeze unit here."

"Oh, that, why," and he looked around nervously, "I'm certain you have at some point or another."

Her voice was low and certain. "I can assure, you, Dr. Rochelle, I would recall seeing such a unit. Where is it?"

"Why, it's—"

At that moment they were interrupted by coarse laughter punctuating a string of profanity. Seconds later Gunn entered the lab, pulling along the now-handcuffed Abby. In his right hand he was holding the handle of a small box Lana recognized as the portable freezer unit Arcane had sent out with them. It was Abby who was cursing, naturally, and Gunn who was laughing.

Behind them, strolling casually as if he had all the time in the world, was Arcane. "Now, now," he scolded, "I thought, Abigail, your mother had taught you better. Such language."

"Up yours," she snarled, and looked around at the lab. "Oh, great. And this must be the playroom. I have to say, no crazed scientist should be without one." Her face tightened. "You may have stopped Alec, but he'll be back. And he may have looked like a monster, but he had the mind and feelings of a man. You're the exact opposite."

"Stopped him?" Rochelle was saying nervously. "Dr. Arcane, I hate to bring this up, but we still need a sample of Holland's tissue for the locking serum we're going to make." He turned to Abby and explained, as if she cared. "Without the right ingredients for the formula, your stepfather's body will eventually deteriorate."

"Yes," Arcane echoed, smiling at Lana. "I will deteriorate."

"Like your mind," shot back Abby.

"Don't get yourself in an uproar, Dr. Frankenstein," said Gunn cheerily, and he tossed the small unit to Rochelle. "We scraped that off the propeller blade that made coleslaw out of 'im. Should be more than enough."

Rochelle stared in through the clear, albeit frosted, top. "Oh, yes," he said excitedly. "Yes, indeed."

"Take Abigail to our holding center," said Arcane easily, feeling utterly confident. "We should be ready for her in a bit."

Gunn started to do as ordered when Abigail suddenly planted her feet and said, "My mother, you creep."

Arcane raised a curious eyebrow. "Yes? What about her?"

"How did she fit into all of this?"

Arcane sighed deeply and folded his hands behind his back. "Developing a restoration drug over many years is a very demanding process. Your mother worked with us, as an assistant. . . ."

"Or as a guinea pig?" snapped Abby.

He inclined his head slightly. "Semantics. Her death was an unfortunate side effect of our mutual experiments." He walked toward her slowly, stopping several feet away. "Her genetic code was perfect . . . just like yours."

It took a moment for it to sink in. "You're . . . you're going to do to me . . . what you did to my mother."

"Her death was inadvertent, even tragic. Perhaps you will be more fortunate."

"You son of a bitch!" she shrieked. "All your talk about how you loved her! How you cared about her! It was all just bullshit, wasn't it? *Wasn't it?*"

He stepped forward quickly and slapped her across the face. "I loved your mother," he said hotly, "as much as I have ever loved anyone. As much as I can love anyone. You have no idea what she meant to me. Even after her death, I never let her go. What becomes mine, remains mine, for eternity."

Her cheek stinging, she fought back tears. "What the hell are you talking about?"

He stared at her for a moment, then with brisk steps walked over to the wall and slid aside a panel Lana Zurrell had never noticed before to reveal an array of colored switches. Arcane flipped the one in the upper left-hand corner.

Hidden motors whirred, and to Lana's astonishment, part of the wall slid back to reveal a six-foot-tall upright container. A blast of cold emanated from it, and she realized the inside of the container was completely encrusted with ice.

No. Not completely.

Two-thirds of the way up, there was a clear spot: peering through it was a face.

The face resembled Abby's. It's eyes were wide open in a rictus of horror. Icicles hung from its eyebrows; its skin was blue; its frost-covered lips slightly parted as though about to speak. It stared at the world lifelessly.

"My dear," Arcane said in a conversational tone, "you have a visitor. See?" He gestured toward Abby. "It's your daughter. See how she's grown? Isn't she beautiful? As beautiful as you were."

Abby's mouth moved, but no words came out. Over in the corner, Lana Zurrell jammed a fist into her own mouth to prevent a scream.

"You see, Abby?" Arcane said proudly. "I did love her. I still do. No one can ever replace her in my heart. I shall love her forever. Of course, unfortunately . . ."—he smiled gently—"you always kill the one you love."

Lana shut her eyes and heard her own scream echoing in her head, except it was coming from Abby. The scream went on and on, and she bit her lips until they bled to prevent her own scream from mingling.

She came very close to blacking out. Suddenly she felt a touch at her cheek and jumped slightly. She opened her eyes, and Arcane was there, smiling at her.

She looked around. Abby was gone. The frozen body of Abby's mother was gone. Only the terror remained.

"I'm sorry, my dear," he said softly. "I should have considered your feelings. That was probably something of a shock to you."

Lana drew an unsteady breath and forced a

smile. "After everything I've seen, you'd think nothing would shock me."

"Yes. Now . . . I am feeling fatigued. I shall go rest before the operation. You assist Dr. Rochelle in the final preparations. And then, after the operation . . ."—he patted her cheek fondly—"we shall celebrate as never before."

He turned and walked out of the lab, and Lana watched him go, feeling completely, utterly numb.

He had no idea, she realized. He had absolutely no idea how he, or anything he said or did, affected her.

She felt as if her mind were beginning to clear. Whatever magic he had used on her—personal magnetism, charm, hypnotism—whatever it had been that had attracted her to him, that had made her his virtual slave, was beginning to lose its potency. Perhaps he hadn't reckoned on her strength of will. Perhaps he had simply become overconfident and hadn't counted on the effects his acts would have on her.

Rochelle's soft voice behind her made her jump.

"Dr. Zurrell?" he said. "I need your help in this."

"Oh?" she replied, trying to put together a course of action. She stared at this horrid man with whom she'd worked and felt a wave of nausea.

"I need to draw a small amount of blood from

you," he said, his hands fidgeting. "Just as a test, you understand."

"What about . . ." She licked her dry lips. "What about Conklin?"

"Well . . ." Rochelle sighed. "If I take any more I'm afraid I might kill him. Still, we can check his levels, I suppose."

He now went to the same panel Arcane had been at moments before and flicked a different switch. This time another wall panel opened and Conklin, in a similar compartment but one not covered with ice, slid out. He was blanched, almost completely drained of blood.

"I would really hate for him to die," said Rochelle unhappily. "I had something very special planned for him. I even had a special cage prepared." He pointed over toward a darkened corner of the lab.

"Really?"

"Yes," said Rochelle, warming to his subject. He started over toward the cage. "Believe me, its potential exceeds anything we've attempted thus far. I've developed a pyridoxine hydrochloric emulsion that, when combined with a human pituitary extract, will produce a nearly spontaneous superdeveloped mutation." He pointed toward a solution in a labeled vial in a test tube rack. Then he paused and smiled. "Remember that evolved man with a superbig head in *The Outer Limits*? That's where I got the idea from."

"Wouldn't you be risking cranial hypertrophy?" Lana stopped next to a microscope on a nearby table.

"Nothing wrong with that" was his cheerful reply. He opened the cage and reached in, pointing proudly. "Now you can see where I've reinforced the—"

He never completed the sentence, since the microscope crashed down across the back of his head. He went to his knees, tried to stagger up, and Lana brought it down a second time, knocking him cold.

She shoved him all the way into the cage and checked his skull. He might have had a concussion.

"Nothing wrong with that": she echoed his words. Then she realized there *was* something wrong with that. It wasn't enough. Not nearly enough for the little bloodsucker.

She glanced around at the test tube he had so proudly indicated moments ago. She smiled mirthlessly, and, dusting herself off, went to begin preparing a hypodermic.

The pain . . . of humanity . . .

I had forgotten . . . what it was like.

Earth mother . . . I cannot go out there again . . . and face that.

Why must it be like that? Why must there always be pain . . . when humans are involved?

The flame brought back memories . . . long buried . . . and traumatic. It sent me screaming back to the womb . . . to the cool earth . . . to hide . . . and cower.

But Abby needs me. I can feel her.

She has taken root . . . within me . . . and I cannot deny her . . . for it would be . . . to deny myself.

I am coming . . . Abby. The ghost of Alec Holland . . . is coming to save you . . . and to put . . . other, evil ghosts . . . to rest.

15

The holding cell had been carefully prepared for, and frequently used by, the less enthusiastic guests of the Arcane Mansion in the past.

Now it was Abigail Arcane who sat inside the stark cell, staring with a dull look at the wall. There was some obscene graffiti scrawled on it that didn't even register.

The cell door was heavy wrought iron with an intricate *A* carved in it.

Abby ran her fingers through her hair and brushed against the rose Alec had given her. She sighed slowly, trembling, trying to bring back to herself the feelings she had shared with him.

She heard a nasty chuckle and glanced at her current jailer. Johnny Gunn was seated outside, tilting his chair against the corridor wall.

"So, city girl," he said, snickering, "how'd your 'date' with the swamp man go?"

"None of your business."

Slowly he got up and walked toward the door. "Suppose I make it my business."

"You couldn't begin to understand."

"Yeah? 'Splain it to me, reaaaallll ssssloooowwww."

She stared at him as if studying a microbe.

"So, did you do it with him?" he asked again.

Why should I feel ashamed? "Yeah, I did it with him," she said, getting to her feet. "You got a problem with that?"

He shook his head. "Jeez. You got more problems than I do, lady."

"And why is that? For your information, I happen to love him, okay?"

He gestured widely. "You love him? Christ almighty! I love the salad bar at Wendy's, but you don't see me taking it to dinner and a show!"

She turned away from him, staring sullenly at the ground.

"You don't get it, do ya, city girl? I'm tryin' to be nice to you."

And slowly it started to dawn on her.

She mumbled something softly enough to prompt him to ask, "What was that?"

"I said," she said a bit more loudly, with a heavy sigh as if unburdening herself, "it's probably because I never met a man who could . . . y'know . . . satisfy me."

It hit him exactly where she thought it would: in the ego.

He hitched up his pants slightly and lit up another cigarette before saying, "That a fact?"

She glanced at him over her shoulder coyly. "Uh huh." Then slowly she walked to the door and ran a finger across the bars. "Y'know . . . I know you're trying to be nice to me. I'd be nice to you, too . . . except it's tough behind bars."

Slowly he dangled the cell key in front of her. She watched, not saying a word. He gestured for her to step back, and she did so, eyes never wavering.

He unlocked the door and stepped in before she could get past him. "Where you think you're going?" he asked.

"Thought we'd walk around a little."

"Y'want parole, is that it?"

"Something like that," she said nervously.

"Well, then . . . first y'gotta show good behavior. So let's see how good you can be." He moved toward her slowly and was pleased to see she wasn't backing away. "C'mon, city girl, let's play doctor."

She smiled back. "Sure thing, sweets. Bet'cha can't guess my favorite operation."

Grinning, he said, "What's that, baby?"

She suddenly dropped to the ground and lashed out in a vicious side kick that caught Gunn square in the groin. He sank to one knee, gasping.

"A vasectomy, asshole," she snapped, and bolted for the door.

She hadn't counted on Gunn recovering as quickly as he did. He lunged, grabbing her wrist, and he staggered to his feet as he dragged her back. She tried to struggle, but he was holding her arms tight at her sides. Breathing in her ear he spat out, "Like that? Ten years training in Okinawa."

He swung her around, blocking her knee with his leg, and kissed her harshly. He pulled back, grinning, and Abby viciously slammed her forehead into his nose. He let out a yell, putting a hand against her face to shove her head back, and she sank her teeth into him, drawing blood.

She pulled away from him, interlaced her fingers, and swung with all her strength. The rabbit punch landed squarely on the side of his head, dropping him like a rock.

"Like that?" she shot back. "Two days of vacation in East L.A."

She turned, ran for the door, shoved through, dashed into the hallway, and got exactly five paces before Points dropped her with a right hook to the jaw.

Abby lay there, the ceiling spinning around, and she rubbed her throbbing jaw. Points hauled Abby to her feet as Gunn staggered out of the cell, still shaking off the effects of the ear blow he'd received.

Abby tried to refocus and saw half a dozen security men in the hallway. Gunn's short laugh resounded behind her.

"You thought I'd go in the cell with you without having backup handy?" he demanded, shaking his head once more to clear it. "City girl, you must think I'm some sort of major idiot."

Flexing her jaw once more to restore it to life,

she said, "No, I didn't think they promoted you past corporal idiot."

The other guards chuckled, but Gunn silenced them with an angry stare.

"Get her down to the lab. Arcane should be ready for her." As they started to haul her off down the hallway, he called after her, "Hey, city girl! Maybe we'll get together in the next lifetime!"

And she shouted back, "Maybe! When I come back as a human, and you come back as a cockroach, I'll make sure to step on you!"

"Wear high heels!"

He laughed, and was cut off by a scream.

He stared at Points.

"Damned if that didn't sound like Arcane."

Arcane sat bolt upright in his bed, his body covered in sweat, having awakened from a nightmare that had a sense of imminence to it.

He rolled off, fell once, staggered to his feet, and ran to the intercom. "Gunn!"

Obediently the security head's voice came over the speaker. "Right here. You have a bad dream or something?"

"I'm living it. Bring Abby down to the lab."

"Already being done."

"Make sure Rochelle is ready."

"I'll have my people look for him. Anything else?"

"Yes." He swallowed. "Holland is coming."

There was a snort of disbelief. "No way. We

quick-fried him. And even if he did come back, he's only hot shit when there's plants and stuff around. There isn't a lick of green in this whole joint. Not on the grounds, not in—"

"I don't care!" he shouted. "Make preparations. I'll be right down."

He released the talk button and leaned against the wall.

"Not this time, Holland," he whispered, his body trembling. "Not this time."

Through the great bay window of the main study, Arcane and Lana were surveying the perimeter of the area. The vast expanse of concrete provided some measure of satisfaction to Arcane. Still, it was difficult to anticipate everything. Was there anything he had overlooked? The samples taken from Holland's body had been completely used up in developing the compound, the vitality sucked from them and the remains burned, so that would be of no help to him.

The experiment was going as planned. Everything would be perfect . . .

Except . . . there was something nagging at the back of his mind. Lately, as the deterioration had accelerated, it had been harder to think, harder to hold any thought for enough time to draw conclusions. There was something he was overlooking; he was certain. But what?

Gunn walked up to him and tossed off another mock salute. "I've got sensors all over the property. If anything breaks through those beams, we'll know it."

"Good," said Arcane without looking away from the perimeter. "Have you located Dr. Rochelle yet?"

"My people swear he's on the grounds, but no one's seen him."

Arcane bristled. "We need him for the operation."

There was a reassuring touch on his arm. "Don't worry, darling," Lana said softly. "I'm fully capable of carrying on without the doctor."

He looked down at her. She smiled lovingly, his obedient servant. "Of course you are." He touched her chin. "Begin the preparations. I'll be along in a moment."

"Certainly."

She walked away as Arcane turned to Gunn and spoke in a stern whisper: "Find Rochelle."

"Ten-Four, Doc." He turned as Points was entering the room and quickly gestured for her to follow.

Arcane took one last look out at the swamp.

The combatant would be coming for him.

" 'Lay on, Macduff,' " he whispered fiercely, " 'And damned be him that first cries "Hold, enough!" ' "

I do not have to see your gaze . . . to feel your evil . . . Arcane.

You poison . . . all you touch . . . you . . . and all your hellspawn allies . . . must be cleansed . . . from the earth.

Humans think nothing . . . of defoliating entire forests . . . in the name of war. This is war, Arcane . . . nothing less than war . . . and this time . . . the foliage is striking back.

16

Sheriff Beaumont walked slowly into the lobby of the Wein Motel, glancing automatically at the now vacant corner where that G-man had appeared determined to take up permanent residence.

"Where'd he go?" he asked.

From behind the counter Alan looked up. "He made some arrests and felt he at least had something to show for the horror that went on in there. Ask me now, I don't think two producers of cheap alcohol balance the scales for the loss of four lives. Then again, I just work here."

"Uh huh." He started for the door.

"I wouldn't," said Alan calmly.

Beaumont paused and turned to look at the long-haired clerk. "Wouldn't what?"

"Were you considering going to the Arcane Mansion?"

"Uh huh, yeah. Just thought I might do a little follow-up." He grinned and traced a woman's curve in the air. "Check out the scenery, if ya catch my drift."

"Consider it caught. Now catch this: Save your little sojourn for tomorrow. Stay away from it tonight."

He walked slowly toward Alan, blinking in confusion. "Why? You think there's going to be some kind of little trouble up there?"

"That depends."

"Depends on what?"

"On how you define 'little trouble.' For example, would you consider when God, in his wrath, smote the cities of Sodom and Gomorrah, that was 'little trouble'?"

Beaumont considered that a moment. "That was big trouble."

"Indeed. Well, then . . . tonight the Arcane Mansion can expect—"

"Big trouble?"

"Major trouble."

"Fine. I'm going home and watching TV."

"Sound idea."

He turned to leave, then stopped and asked, "How do you know about all these things that are happening in the swamp, anyway?"

Alan smiled beneath his beard. "Heard it on the grape vine."

Abby closed her eyes a moment, praying when she opened them, the scene would change. She did. It didn't.

She was still down in Arcane's lab, strapped to

a chair that seemed as if it were from the office of a rather sadistic dentist. Next to her was a large, rotating device that looked like some sort of mixing device, glistening metal and ugly. On the other side of the device was a chair identical to the one she sat in.

Lana came into the operating room from the lab section. She stopped, taking a deep breath as if to compose herself.

"Please," Abby said in a low voice, "help me. I know you hate my guts, but—"

"I don't," Lana said quietly. "I'm too tired to hate anymore. There's nothing further I can do. There's simply no escape from here."

"What will he do to me?"

What point was there in mincing words? "The same thing he did to your mother." She came closer and in a harsh whisper said, "I'd set you free if I thought you'd get farther than the front door."

"I'm game if you are," said Abby, trying to keep her flagging hopes up.

Then came the sound of the elevator arriving in the other room, the door opening, followed by the rapid footsteps Abby had already come to know and loathe.

Arcane entered, dressed in shimmering white. He stopped, surveyed the scene, and smiled. He moved closer to Abby. "You know, my dear, I'm very glad you and Holland got along so well. Very soon you'll be very, very close to each other."

She said nothing, glowering at him with pure

venom. Almost longingly he touched her hair. She twisted her head away as far as she was able.

"Let me explain. Genes. Yours," and he held out one hand, fingers outstretched, "Holland's . . ." and he held out the other, then interlaced the fingers. ". . . coupled . . . and man's oldest dream may come true." He smiled. "Immortality."

"You're sick," shot back Abby. "What did you do? Sell yourself to the devil?"

He inclined his head slightly. "Let's just say he has a lease with an option to buy."

In a cage in the corner of the lab, something stirred.

In the swamp, near the edge of the fence, something stirred.

Farther back in the swamp, deep in the rushes, something stirred.

"I'm going stir-crazy waiting around," snarled Gunn as he and Points stalked into Arcane's study. He glanced around at the shelves and shelves of books, but his attention was held even longer by the assortment of antique weapons, the sabers, the daggers, the elegant pistols and such. "Damn," he continued. "I was wrong. I was sure we'd find Rochelle lost in his books here again."

"Gunn," said Points in bemusement, sitting on a table and swinging her legs insouciantly, "your ignorance is exceeded only by your incompetence."

"Thanks, Points. And your IQ's exceeded only by your bra size. Or maybe it's even-steven, I can't be sure."

"Make all the smart-ass remarks you want," she said. "Some head of security. You're not smart enough to be a head of beer. Real soon now, I'll have your job."

"No way. You try to take my job," said Gunn, "all you'll get is a scar," and he drew an imaginary line from ear to ear, "from here to here."

"You can't scare me," replied Points, her eyes flashing. "See this?" She lifted up the hair from the back of her neck, exposing a scar from side to side. "The guy who did this to me—I got his job, too."

He took a step toward her and whistled. "That is a nasty scar. But it's nothing compared to this." He pulled down his shirt from the shoulder, displaying an angry-looking wound. "Grenada, 1983. Friendly fire."

Points snorted. "That's bush, compared to this—" She raised her shirt to reveal a whiplike red scar on her lower back. "Falkland Islands, 1982. Shrapnel."

Gunn paused and then cracked his knuckles, as if engaging in major battle. He yanked his shirt to one side, showing an ugly rip across his chest. "Nicaragua—spring break '87."

In retaliation in what was rapidly escalating into Scar Wars, Points posed sexily revealing a wound between her armpit and back. "Beirut—summer vacation '88."

Gunn paused, suddenly realizing he'd run out of battle scars. In desperation he displayed his belly and pointed to what had become the faintest of white lines. "Appendix—Haight-Ashbury General Hospital—1967 . . . the summer of *looove.*"

At that Points suppressed an outright laugh, and ripped open the seam of her leggings, revealing bite marks on her thigh. Her voice defiant and triumphant, she declared, "Motley Crue tour—1989!"

They were now inches from each other, major portions of their flesh displayed, their blood pumping both from the nonsensical showdown and the thought of imminent battle, and they started to reach for each other.

Hugo smashed in through the doors.

"Doesn't anybody *knock* around here?!" yelled Gunn.

"We've spotted the Swamp Thing, sir! He's headed this way!"

"Put everyone on full alert. And next time knock for chrissakes!"

Abby, still strapped in her chair, watched fearfully as Lana assisted Arcane in activating a massive bank of electric and biomedical systems. Liquid pumps and electromagnets pulsed to life. Several clear hoses networked out from the side of the large machine near her, and ended at a clear canister resting between two receptors.

Arcane stepped past Abby and, insanely, tipped an imaginary hat. He sat down in front of a video monitor and flipped more switches as, nearby, Lana lined up readings on several gauges.

The machine next to Abby started to pulsate.

Suddenly Arcane jumped in alarm at the sound of running feet. Seconds later Points ran in.

"Problem," said Points. "The creeping crud is headed our way."

Behind him, Swamp Thing had left a torn fence. In his left hand he carried a large chunk of the chain link. In his right hand was a six-foot-long fence post.

He walked with slow, measured strides, his moist feet making plopping noises on the alien concrete. He surveyed the territory in front of him, the vast, plain expanse, and if he could not sneak up on them, the advantage was that they could not sneak up on him.

The problem was that he was not standing on dirt, and therefore could not draw bodily replenishment from the earth. What he had would have to do.

He heard the bullets before he saw the people, shouts of "There he is!" and "Get him!"

Bullets began to pepper him, pierce his body harmlessly but taking with them clods of dirt.

There were half a dozen of them bearing down on him. Fine.

He started to pick up speed, heading toward them like an avalanche, and he let out an inhuman scream that chilled them to the bone. Then he drew back his arm and hurled the chain link at them.

They scrambled to get out of its way but were not terribly successful. It dropped down on them, pinning several of them underneath. By the time they managed to pull themselves together, Swamp Thing was in the midst of them, swinging the fence post like a knight wading into his enemies with a broadsword.

There was no mercy in him for those who had aided in Abby's abduction. He crushed the skulls of two, caved in the ribs of a third, and when he slammed the jagged bottom of the post forward, came close to disemboweling a fourth. A fifth man, thinking range would have some effect, came in tight with his automatic and fire point-blank into Swamp Thing's chest. The creature's response was to crush the gun, along with the hand holding it.

The sixth man backpedaled furiously to get some distance as he pulled a hand grenade from his bandolier. Swamp Thing picked up one of the fallen security men and hurled him at the retreating one. They went down in a tangle of arms and legs, the grenade rolling away with the pin unpulled. The man tried to scramble to his feet, but a casual swing of Swamp Thing's massive fist snapped his head around, knocking him out.

A *fwooof* sound came from a distance, and suddenly Swamp Thing darted to one side as a round of bazooka fire landed right where he had been standing.

Many yards away, an SP7 mounted on his massive shoulder, Hugo howled with joy and took aim again. He let fly, and this time Swamp Thing literally had to hit the deck to avoid the hurling missile. It struck the fence behind him and exploded.

To his left Swamp Thing spotted the unused grenade. He grabbed it up.

"A pineapple. How appropriate," he rumbled as he pulled the pin and hurled it.

From his great distance, Hugo saw the muck monster make the distinctive throwing gesture of someone heaving a grenade. He laughed to himself. No way was it going to make it all the way to where he was: it was way too far. No one could throw it that distance: one needed a grenade launcher.

He thought that up until the moment the grenade landed at his feet. It was also the last thought he had.

"Lana . . ." Arcane pointed toward a rack of clear canisters filled with different samples of liquids and oozes. "The Holland specimen. Put it in the receptor."

As Lana moved toward it, Points said urgently, "I'm telling you, Swamp Thing's coming."

"No one appreciates the gravity of the situation more than I do. You must stop him. We need more time." He moved toward a large carrying rack with glass vials. "Use these. It's a by-product of Agent Orange."

The words CORROSIVE ACID were all Points had to see. She smiled.

As Points walked out with the tubes, Arcane flipped open a panel next to the transformation device, revealing a row of lighted switches. Within moments he had started the two chairs, Abby's and the unoccupied one, rotating.

Desperately Abby said, "Think about what you're doing."

"Believe me, I am." There was a momentary gleam in his eyes. "Abby, you're about to experience a unique feeling. You're about to be part of what brings life."

"To you!" she cried out.

He nodded. "To me." Then he smiled that mirthless smile. "It's for a good cause."

Now the mansion was in sight, and Swamp Thing seethed with frustration at the amount of time it was all taking.

There seemed to be no further obstructions. It was simple. Too simple.

He arrived at the front of the mansion, started up the steps . . .

The porch exploded.

The Swamp Thing was hurled back, bits of him scattered all about. He lay on the ground, dazed, looked up at the rapidly disappearing sun, and then rolled over and began to literally pull himself together. He grabbed up pieces of dirt and stuck them back on, gathered up fistfuls of leaves and mud.

What had caused the explosion?

He didn't have long to wait for an answer. There was a jubilant war cry behind him, and he spun in time to see Gunn, driving a Jeep full tilt in his direction. An unlit cigarette hanging from the corner of his mouth, Gunn was cackling furiously.

It was easy to see why: A powerful rocket launcher cannon was attached to each fender, one of which had just been fired and was still smoking. Not only that, but an imposing M60 machine gun was mounted next to the driver's side, allowing Gunn to maneuver with one hand and target Swamp Thing with the other.

"Have some croutons!" he shouted, blasting away with the machine guns.

Swamp Thing staggered under the barrage, dodging some bullets, getting hit by more. As Gunn sped by, Swamp Thing sank to his knees, shaking his head and trying to reorient himself.

"No so tough without plants around, are ya!" shouted Gunn. The brakes screeched as he slammed the Jeep around and started back toward the Swamp Thing once more.

The muck monster looked up with his blazing red eyes, looked at his enemy closely, reached out with his mind.

Gunn was about to start firing again when Swamp Thing spoke, and he held off a moment to hear what the creature said.

"Don't you know . . ." he rumbled in a voice

from beyond the grave, "that cigarettes . . . are bad for you . . . ?"

Gunn didn't have the faintest idea what he was talking about. Then his cigarette came alive.

The tobacco grew wildly, stretching out and breaking through the paper. In seconds the tobacco had spread, covering Gunn's face, blocking his vision, shoving its way up his nostrils, into his ears, and down his screaming mouth.

Totally forgetting he was in a Jeep barreling along at better than fifty miles per hour, Gunn frantically clawed at the berserk cancer stick. He lost control of the Jeep and, for good measure, the Swamp Thing kicked it as it shot by.

The force of the blow sent it spinning toward the mansion and, seconds later, the Jeep erupted into a fireball.

Swamp Thing stepped back, shading his eyes, and tried to make out whether or not Gunn had been thrown clear.

At that second he was assaulted by machine gun fire.

More security guards, with Points in the lead, were pouring from the door of the mansion.

They are worse than locusts . . . these humans . . . multiplying at phenomenal rates . . . and eating away at me . . . and at the time.

Abby is in danger . . . and I am wasting time . . . thinking in two-dimensional terms. Fighting the humans . . . is clumsy and inefficient. There must be a better way.

I reach out . . . seeking some means of entry . . . into the mansion.

I sense plant life . . . microscopic, bacteria . . . traces of mold . . . millions of infinitesimal organisms . . . individually so humble . . . beneath the notice of all . . . but me.

They are beneath my feet . . . flowing into the mansion . . . where I wish to be.

I am coming . . . Abby.

Points watched in astonishment as the Swamp Thing's body crumbled in a heap.

Someone shouted, "We did it! He's dead!"

"Like hell he is!" shot back Points. "He must have gone *some*where. What's right beneath us?"

"Nothing! Well, maybe pipes, but that's—"

"The plumbing!" shrieked Points. "He's in the goddamn plumbing! Back in the house, quick!"

And as they dashed back in after the elusive swamp creature, a hulking, broken form huddled back by the fence and began to make its slow way across the compound.

I flow with the water . . . riding it to my destination . . . and seek out some outlet . . . through which I can emerge.

Within seconds . . . I have located a dripping faucet . . . and I begin to draw together components . . . to grow a body. The water turns thick with sludge . . . slowly filling the bathtub . . . not the most aesthetic body . . . but certainly serviceable.

I am . . . piping myself in. Certainly Abby would appreciate . . . the humor in that.

Abby . . .

It was as if he were in a giant centrifuge. With each turn of the chair into which he was strapped, Arcane began to feel healthier, stronger. The skin began to smooth out and become strong and vibrant; the gray in his hair disappeared, replaced by youthful black.

He had been concerned when Rochelle had misplaced himself, but he now knew his worries had been needless. Lana was handling matters with thoroughly professional aplomb.

Lana, for her part, was not watching Arcane at all. She could not take her eyes off the whirling figure of Abby whose eyes were half-closed, her skin visibly wilting.

Through cracked lips she called out in a voice barely above a whisper, "Please . . . don't let him kill me . . . like he did my mom. . . ."

"He did not kill your mother," Lana replied briskly. "Rochelle did that. Dr. Arcane was merely the temporary beneficiary."

Arcane was paying no heed to what was being said. He was busy reveling in the power and strength flowing into him. "I feel very good," he whispered, "very good. The energy . . . the energy . . . it's extraordinary."

"Dosage up to 2 ccs per minute," Lana called out. "Temperature holding at 98.2. Heartbeat at 98. Nervous system showing improvement."

"Increase the dosage," he called, and then more forcefully, "Increase the dosage! How beautiful!"

Abby closed her eyes and felt her life being drained away.

I lose . . . some of myself . . . down the drain . . . but quickly reconstitute more . . . and within moments . . . I step from the bathtub . . . and look around . . . at the ornately tiled room.

I look down at the toilet . . . and consider that I could have emerged . . . from there. Oddly . . . that would have seemed . . . undignified somehow.

I go to the door . . . open it . . . and watch my body begin to burn away.

The canister containing the mixture of Abby's blood and the distillation of Alec Holland was nearly empty.

As Arcane watched with anticipation, Lana heard shouting from overhead. "We've got to hurry," she said urgently.

"Not yet," said Arcane.

In her chair, Abby tried to raise her head at the noise. "Alec?" she said weakly. Then she slumped back, unable to move.

The rose the Swamp Thing had given her, what seemed a lifetime ago, fell from her hair and dropped to the floor, where it lay forlornly.

"Alec," she whispered again. "Oh, God, Alec . . . where in hell are you?"

• • •

The guards had split up into teams of two, and Points and her partner were fortunate enough to be there when the Swamp Thing emerged from the bathroom in Arcane's own bedroom.

She had the test tubes ready and, realizing this might be her only shot, hurled the entire rack against him.

The Agent Orange by-product ate away greedily at the Swamp Thing's body. He staggered under the assault, but had no chance at all. He lurched to one side, his legs giving way as the corrosive acid burned away all support. He tried to speak but his jaw dropped off.

"Don't get too close!" shouted Points as she drew her automag and started firing at his head.

Abby . . . they won't let up . . . and I'm failing you. Where are you? I need to find you.

There . . . I feel it now.

I'm coming . . . Abby.

The other guards arrived just in time to see Points blow apart his skull. Bits of him were still sizzling on the carpet, and his lifeless eye sockets stared up at them.

"That's it," said Points. "That's gotta be it. Where the hell else is he going to go?"

Arcane, having unstrapped himself from the chair, was now standing and staring into the lab mirror suspended overhead. Slowly he nodded in admiration, running his fingers across his flesh.

"Not bad," he said. "Not bad at all."

He stretched out his hands, admiring the backs of them . . .

And they began to wrinkle . . .

And large pieces started to peel off . . . and the pieces fell to the floor and crumbled into dust. . . .

Arcane could not believe it. Would not believe it.

"What's happening?" It was a hoarse whisper, then a high-pitched scream of alarm. "What's happening?!"

He dashed to the machine, skidding on the highly polished floor, and began checking the readings. Fine.

He checked the couplings. Fine.

He grabbed up the container that held the Holland mixture.

Not fine.

Now the faintest of whispers, he read the label. "Subject #3-11-459."

With slow, deadly menace he turned toward Lana. "You switched the vials," he said incredulously, unable to cope with the reality. "You switched the vials."

Lana started to back away slowly, drifting toward the secret exit from the lab that only she, Arcane, and Rochelle knew about. "It was the only way," she said, fighting to keep panic from her voice. "You were going to kill me. . . ."

"Am going to kill you," he corrected, and with a swift, sure movement he pulled a revolver from inside his beautiful white jacket and fired at Lana.

The bullet struck her just above the heart, spinning her back and away from him. She fell to the floor, clutching at the bullet hole, trying to stanch the blood fountaining from the wound.

"God will forgive me," he intoned. "That's his job." He advanced on her, shaking his head in disappointment. "Without the biorestorative formula from Holland's body, there's no stopping the deterioration."

Then a low, taunting laugh from Abby brought him up short. "You . . . idiot . . ." she said.

He turned on her, Lana momentarily forgotten. "What do you mean?" he said in a deadly voice.

"I should . . . have realized," Abby said weakly, her strength ebbing. "Even if it had been the right stuff . . . it wouldn't have done any good. Alec . . . has regrown his body over and over. . . . The precious formula isn't in his body anymore. . . . He's moved beyond that." She smiled, content in Arcane's failure. "That's the difference . . . stepdad—good grows and evolves . . . while evil just feeds on itself. . . ."

"No." He shook his head slowly. "It . . . it couldn't have been for nothing."

"How about that?" she said. "I'm starting to see things . . . like Alec does."

I find it.
Abby . . . I'm here.

The rose that had fallen to the floor began to grow.

From one stem grew a hundred; from a dozen thorns sprang a thousand.

Arcane watched in dull terror as the Swamp Thing took form, fashioning a body from the rose. The stems intertwined, the thorns grew long and dangerous and, incongruously, petals blossomed all over him.

Within short moments he was standing there, staring at Arcane with all the hatred in his being.

"That's a good style for you," said Arcane calmly.

All but forgotten, Lana Zurrell had gotten to the secret passage. She dragged herself up the stairs one agonizing step at a time, leaving a trail of blood behind her.

I will live, she told herself. If I can just stop the bleeding, I'll live.

She found the door, the door, which, from the outside, fitted so smoothly with the exterior of the house, it was impossible to distinguish. She shoved it once, but it didn't budge. She threw herself against it a second time, and this time it opened.

She staggered out into the night, the exertion causing the blood to flow even faster.

She fell to the concrete, ripping her skin, and lay there, praying the bleeding would stop.

She heard a footfall near her.

I'm saved, she thought.

She twisted herself around and looked into the inhuman eyes of a blackened and broken mass that at one time had been Wong Sing Bernstein, psychiatrist and acupressurist.

The Leech had refused to die, had clung on stubbornly to life in order to find, one final time, that beautiful image that had sprung to its mind.

"Oh, God . . . no," she said.

Its maw moved, making unholy noises, and it finally found its voice.

"Lawww . . . naaa . . . I . . . luhhve . . . yoouuu."

She closed her eyes and surrendered as it brought its mouth to her wound.

The bleeding stopped.

Swamp Thing turned his gaze on Abby's unmoving form and went berserk.

He grabbed up a chair and hurled it at Arcane. It smashed into the scientist's chest, driving him back toward the darkened corner of the lab. He fell directly in front of the specially reinforced cage Rochelle had created.

The Swamp Thing let out an inhuman roar, which was met by a challenging roar from within the cage.

The door exploded outward, landing on Arcane and pinning him underneath.

What had once been Dr. Rochelle emerged from the cage.

His head was now hairless and huge, the sides pulsing. His eyes were no more than large black pupils. He swung a long-fingered hand around, inadvertently hitting the volume switch for the caged "manimals." The he uttered incomprehensible noises and charged at the Swamp Thing with incredible speed.

Swamp Thing took a glance at Abby, saw she was sinking, and then had no more time as he met the charge of the mutated Rochelle.

Now all the other mutated creatures began to scream and shout and bellow in excitement from their cages, sensing distantly that one of these creatures had been their tormentor . . . sensing, perhaps, that at last he was overmatched.

Rochelle smashed himself into Swamp Thing and let out a scream. He leapt back, blood flowing from a dozen cuts.

For a moment the Swamp Thing didn't fully understand what had happened, and then he looked down and did understand. He was covered with thorns. He was a devastating weapon.

Rochelle tried a feint.

No chance.

He tried to come in fast. He tried bobbing and weaving.

No chance.

Every time he came anywhere remotely within striking distance, Swamp Thing lashed out with those deadly fists. He didn't even have to connect directly. A sideswipe with his arm was enough to leave huge gashes in Rochelle's body. And, unlike Swamp Thing, Rochelle couldn't grow anything back.

He started grabbing equipment, his strength at least tripled, and hurled it all at Swamp Thing. The swamp creature knocked each piece aside, never slowing his advance, never lessening his anger.

Slowly, her strength starting to return, Abby opened her eyes weakly. She saw Alec, but she saw something else: a creature wearing Rochelle's clothing, but completely different; something never before seen.

"How about that . . ." she whispered. "New Rochelle . . ."

Rochelle grabbed up the door that pinned Arcane and held it up as a desperate shield. Swamp Thing slammed into it, thorns snapping off against it, and Rochelle felt a brief surge of hope.

It was, however, extremely brief. Swamp Thing shoved the door back, back toward the wall, and within seconds had crushed Rochelle against it. The mutated scientist tried to shove back, grunting and moaning in desperation, and then suddenly Swamp Thing had lifted both the door and Rochelle over his head.

He turned, looking for someplace to hurl his cargo.

And a low, bemused voice spoke up. "How about over there?"

Swamp Thing swung around to stare at the speaker: Arcane. He lay there, legs hopelessly crushed. He was pointing and saying, "Over there is a disintegration chamber. Throw him there. I never liked him anyway, you see."

Alec paused a moment. If Arcane wanted it, it wouldn't be the truth. On the other hand, what did he have to lose? He turned and threw the massive door, along with Rochelle, toward the indicated chamber.

Rochelle smashed into it, the impact setting off the device into a dazzling display of pyrotechnics. Electricity arced through Rochelle, and he screamed as his body sizzled and fried into nothingness. Arcane watched with rapt attention, like a child at a Fourth of July celebration.

The explosions spread to the other machines, one after the other, like dynamite dominoes. The cages of the mutations caught fire and burned, and the elephant creature and the hippo man and all the others started to go up in flames.

Alec paused to glance at them briefly, but it was too late for them. Perhaps that was fortunate, although it was not for him to judge. Abby, on the other hand, could still be saved. With the sharp thorns he sliced right through the straps holding her down.

She tried to stand up, and he reached out to help her. She shrieked in pain.

"Watch that!"

"I . . . am sorry. I did not have . . . a thing to wear. . . ."

Sagging against the chair, she looked up in astonishment. "Alec . . . you actually tried to make a joke."

"The operative word . . . is 'tried.' "

The lab now rocked with explosions. Fire erupted all around them, and Swamp Thing fought down a surge of panic.

Through the haze he saw Arcane. Arcane's face

was lined and wrinkled beyond comprehension, the breakdown occurring faster and faster. And he was pointing . . .

Pointing toward what? Abby turned and saw a door, the door Lana Zurrell must have gone through. It was open just a bit, but they could see it and get to it.

"Alec!" she shouted. "This way!"

He followed her out, frustrated that Arcane was clearly beyond his capacity for vengeance.

"Holland" came the fierce whisper. He turned and looked down at the rapidly withering Arcane. "Tell me . . . will you please tell me . . . what it is like to be immortal?"

Perhaps there could be vengeance after all. He said, "No."

Arcane shrieked in frustration, and the Swamp Thing's last view of him before turning away was of Arcane's nose falling off.

He took the lead up the stairs, a still-weak and stumbling Abigail finding a safe place to keep a grip on him. He saw beneath his feet a trail of red. A severely wounded person had clearly used these steps, and only moments before.

"Are you with me?" he asked.

"Forever," she replied.

He felt fresh air filtering down to him and, just ahead, a crack indicating an exit was near. Seconds later they emerged outside the mansion, Abby feeling stronger with every passing moment.

She let out a shriek.

Lana Zurrell lay there, dead white, dead dead. Next to her, wrapped in a perverted lover's embrace, was the Leech. He, too, was dead, a small trace of blood trickling down the side of his face.

"Oh, God . . . Alec . . . what . . . ?"

"Do not ask. It would merely be . . . unpleasant."

"Right."

They started to run from the mansion, concerned that the explosions would spread and possibly take the entire place with them.

The Swamp Thing was in the lead, Abby holding on where she could next to him, and she was saying, "When we finish this business . . . I'm going back to the tree . . . and I'm going to sleep for a year and a ha—"

An explosion interrupted with a loud blast, and at first Swamp Thing thought it had come from the house.

It had not.

Abby released her grip, and he started to tell her to hold on when he saw her pitch forward and land with a sickening thud on the concrete.

He couldn't believe it; it wasn't happening. He rolled her over, certain she was pulling another one of her bizarre jokes. But he looked into her eyes just in time to see the life light disappearing from them. She didn't even have time for a final word.

About thirty yards away from the mansion stood a very singed but very much alive Gunn. Smoke trailed upward from the barrel of his rifle, while a dozen other security guards, including Points, stood nearby.

Blood was beginning to pool on the ground beneath Abby. Swamp Thing looked down at her, then back at her murderer.

"Hey, Green Giant," sneered Gunn. "What's new besides ho-ho-ho?"

17

The Swamp Thing's body began to shake. Great, racking sobs that had no tears gripped him. He crouched down next to Abby, moved her hand, touched her face. The warmth was fading; he could see the light disappearing from her.

A moan began somewhere from within him, and grew louder

(not the light)

and louder

(bring back the light)

and emerged

(PLEASE!)

as a sound none of the humans present would ever forget for the short amount of life they had remaining.

It was the sound the first creature made when the first death was ever felt, the death of every tree ever cut, the death of every animal senselessly slaughtered and butchered, the death of nature, the death of a world, his world—

He screamed, and it carried and echoed and re-echoed, and all through the swamp the creatures stopped making noise and the plants stopped growing and the water stopped flowing, and the swamp joined in mourning and became as one a high, ululating cry of anguish.

The humans shrank back, and they were afraid, or thought they were. Actually, they didn't know what real fear was, not true terror, not the kind that makes you lose complete control and reduces you to a state of mewling infant helplessness. That kind of fear.

But they would learn.

Abby . . .

I have failed you.

I thought like a human . . . and fought like a human . . . and now have only to show for it . . . the human emotion of grief.

I have not begun . . . to tap my true potential . . . to let humanity see . . . what nature can do . . . in its full fury.

A good man died . . . long ago . . . and begged forgiveness for his murderers . . . for they knew not . . . what they did.

But yours . . . knew exactly what they did . . . and there shall be no forgiveness . . . from me.

Alec Holland left his body with such force that it blew apart.

Thorns flew everywhere, ripping through clothes and tearing skin of the guards. Only Abby, lying there like a fairy-tale princess, remained unscathed by the barrage.

Slowly the guards pulled themselves together and looked around at one another, sharing a common surprise that it had been that easy.

"We'll hunt him down," said Gunn. "Wherever he is, we'll find him and finish him. Soon as we get Arcane squared away and see what's wh—"

Points spotted it first.

She pointed, her finger quaking. "LOOK!"

The lesson in fear had begun.

Down in the lab, Arcane endeavored to reattach his nose. Ultimately he decided he was better off without it. No doubt the lab was thick with the stench of frying meat anyway.

He tried to crawl toward the exit, but suddenly the rock walls of the lab began to crack apart. He looked around in shock. Grass was growing out of them, beginning to fill the entire lab.

"Holland," he whispered.

I am the swamp.

I am the land.

It is time . . . they all learn . . . just exactly what that means.

Deep within the green . . . I send out my mind . . . and create a body for myself . . . as none before.

My shoulders are vast . . . my fingers miles long . . . the tallest trees are but specks . . . upon me. My head is majestic . . . and all-seeing . . . and terrible. All the rivers are my veins . . . all the land my body . . . all the vengeance . . . mine.

The mountaintop overlooking the Arcane Mansion now had eyes.

That was what Tasha was pointing at, trembling with fear and terror. Gunn looked up as did the others, and Gunn started to shake his head. "No . . . no, it's a trick. It's gotta be a trick."

The peak reshaped itself, the contours of the trees forming the lines of the Swamp Thing's face. From deep within the mountain were twin glowing red sockets, glaring down at the ants that had presumed to take Abby from him. Boulders and rocks fell away as the mountaintop sculpted itself, creating an avalanche, and within moments it was completed.

It spoke.

"You . . . dare!"

The ground began to rumble beneath them. Concrete broke into huge, jagged shards. Trees and massive vines broke through, climbing upward, twisting together, and forming hands twenty stories tall.

For the first time they comprehended just who and what it was they had transgressed against. But now, of course, it was too late.

Gunn tried to run as a great hand of mud and dirt and stone reached around and grabbed him up. He had time for one shriek of terror before the hand closed, crushing him between its fingers.

They tried to run, but he was everywhere. Some fell beneath great slabs of concrete. Others were suffocated by cascades of rock and dirt. One died of a massive heart attack, and the rest were crushed in the grip of those incomprehensible hands.

Great, green life broke through every stone and fissure of the Arcane Mansion, invading that bastion against nature, filling every inch with grass and trees and brush. Within minutes the mansion had been reclaimed.

And then the Swamp Thing shrugged.

The mansion collapsed in on itself, crashing with a roar, unable to stand even for a moment against the fury of the swamp god who had decided to erase the abomination of Arcane and his people from the face of the earth.

For long minutes afterward the rumbling and the aftershocks continued.

And slowly . . .

. . . slowly . . .

His wrath subsided.

The great red eyes of the mountain went dark.

There was silence for a time then, and then small popping and *splutch*ing sounds.

The Swamp Thing reformed himself from the crevices between the great pieces of concrete. He grew there, next to Abby, who had lain peacefully untouched during the horror that had erupted.

He lifted her up gently in his great, mossy arms. He cradled her, amazed at her lack of weight. How could something that, moments before had been so substantial, now seem nonexistent. She seemed so at peace . . . a peace he would never know.

And without a word, he carried her away, leaving the Arcane Mansion to whatever predators and beasts and bits of vegetation chose to take up residence in its remnants.

18

He laid her down in the bough of the tree that would have been her home. He stroked her cheek tenderly, and he wanted to cry—he wanted to cry so much . . .

He forced moisture from the leaves near his eyes and felt the water trickle down his face. Then, slowly, he shook his head and placed his wet cheek against her face.

He left his body for what he was certain would be the last time.

From a safe distance, Omar softly clicked off several shots. "Got it," he whispered. "They are both sleeping I think."

"All right, let's get outta here," said Darryl. "Where to?"

"Wherever's closest. Man, I'm going to buy me a Corvette with the money we get from this."

"What about me?"

"Get your own Corvette."

• • •

I plunge into the green . . . deeper than I have ever gone . . . down until I am beyond the green . . . beyond the earth . . . and into the blackness of nothingness . . . where I will reside from now on.

Earth mother . . . why?

Why?

I thought . . . I was doing as you wished. I thought you desired . . . that I reclaim . . . my human heritage. Yet now . . . she is gone from me. She whom I love . . . and cherish . . . above all others. How can I return . . . when even to look at humans . . . will be painful beyond words? Answer me.

Why have you forsaken me . . . earth mother?

(What is that?)

Somewhere in the darkness beyond . . . I see a small globe . . . of light . . . and beauty.

It comes closer to me . . . and infuses me . . . with its peace . . . and understanding.

And I begin . . . to comprehend . . . the way . . . and the why.

If I am to be the bridge . . . between humanity and nature . . . then I must remember all that is required . . . to be fully human.

I must know the joy . . . and the tragedy . . . the peace . . . and the conflict.

If I am to understand . . . the miracle and exhilaration of birth . . . then I must understand . . . the full nature of grief . . . at the loss of a loved one.

Once . . . I knew these things . . . but I had buried them . . . deep in the earth . . . in the green . . . for they were too painful . . . and it was so much easier . . . to hide.

But, earth mother . . . I need Abby. Despite all I have learned . . . there will be no joy . . . without her. . . . She is mine . . . and I hers . . . and without her . . . I shall always be . . . no more than a thing.

The globe . . . hovers close to me . . . and radiates the colors . . . of the rainbow . . . and a familiar warmth. I reach out to it . . . and clasp it to my bosom . . . and rejoice.

I shall continue to learn from her . . . and grow to be more human . . . and she shall learn more . . . of nature . . . and perhaps one day . . . humanity and nature . . . will regain the harmony there was . . . at the beginning.

The rose . . . the orchid, in its beauty . . . and completeness . . . the one . . .

Return to me, Abby. Share my life . . . be my life. All I am . . . and ever shall be . . . I give to you . . . forever.

19

Abby opened her eyes slowly, not certain what she expected to see.

She saw Alec looking down at her. He seemed nervous, concerned, until she smiled up at him, and then he returned it.

"Hey, Alec," she whispered, prodding him gently. "Is that a tuber in your pocket, or are you just happy to see me?"

He stroked her face gently. "I . . . am happy to see you."

"What happened? I—" She started to sit up. "This is going to sound strange, but . . . did I die?"

Slowly he nodded.

"Then how . . . what did . . . how . . . ?"

He placed a finger against her lips. "I . . . pulled some strings. Although . . . there may be . . . side effects. . . ."

"If one of the effects is that I wind up at your

side, I can live with that. Unless you're attached to this swinging bachelor life-style?"

"Not necessarily." He smiled.

Omar and Darryl stumbled about in the night until they finally reached the darkened motel. They glanced at each other, and Omar whispered, "It's late. Probably nobody awake."

"I'm awake" came a British voice from the lobby.

They opened the screen door, and the man behind the desk reacted with surprise. "Bloody knob didn't come off! Maybe that's a sign of good things to come. What can I do for you gents?"

"We need a place that develops film. But we don't want to send it out or nothin'," said Omar. "We're not letting this baby out of our sight."

"You happen to be in luck," said the long-haired man. "I have a darkroom in the back. I can handle it for you. Let's see the film."

Quickly Omar wound it back, the opened up the back of the camera.

He stared at it for so long, Darryl looked in as well. "Uh oh."

"You didn't put film in the camera?" said Omar hoarsely.

"Me! You're the photographer" came the indignant response.

"That's right, but it's your camera!"

"Who said I had to load it?"

The boys were now nose-to-nose. "I did!" said Omar.

"No, you just said take the other film out. You didn't say put in a new roll!"

"You've got a Twinkie between your ears, you know that?! We missed getting pictures of the Swamp Thing, and it's all your fault!"

"Shut up, Omie!"

"No, you shut up!"

Chuckling softly to himself, the desk clerk moved away and said, "Nice to know everything's back to abnormal."

I hold her close to me . . . for nothing will ever steal her from me . . . again.

As long as I am with her . . . I shall continue to change and grow . . . and learn.

And as long as she is with me . . . she shall grow as well . . . although perhaps not in the way . . . she presumes.

She chatters lovingly . . . making light comments . . . about my putting down roots in the community . . . and raising sprouts. I nod thoughtfully . . . and reach around . . . and pluck a lovely orchid . . . from between her shoulder blades.

And I am whole.